**He kissed her. A**
**wouldn't ea**

Asia turned her body into his. "Please don't stop."

He paused, not sure if he'd only heard what he wanted to hear.

He stared into her eyes, expecting her to pull away. Instead, her hand reached around his back. He covered her mouth with his, succumbing to its inviting warmth. Up close he inhaled the perfume that bathed her skin. He took his time, accepting the invitation of her mouth partly open in welcome. He'd wanted to kiss those full, sexy lips so many times before, and now he finally was. Their tongues touched in a sensual game of introduction.

She pressed against him, crushing her breasts against his chest. He pulled back for air. His chest heaved. His head spun. She had the same effect on him as the climb up the mountain. Before he had a chance to think, he scooped her in his arms and delivered a kiss that had no regard for the rules of proper behavior. He devoured her, enjoying the soft moan that surfaced from the side of her mouth. His hands slipped under her blouse, craving contact with her skin.

She pushed him away and kissed his neck. When she couldn't get to the place she wanted, she pulled his head back and placed her mouth on the spot near his ear lobe. Her teeth grazed his skin with a tantalizing tease that aroused him to the point of no return.

"You can't be real," he moaned. He kissed her passionately and then pushed back.

"Let's just say the feeling is mutual."

**Books by Michelle Monkou**

Kimani Romance

*Sweet Surrender*
*Here and Now*
*Straight to the Heart*
*No One But You*
*Gamble on Love*
*Only in Paradise*
*Trail of Kisses*

Kimani Press Arabesque

*Open Your Heart*
*Finders Keepers*
*Give Love*
*Making Promises*
*Island Rendezvous*

---

## MICHELLE MONKOU

became a world traveler at the age of three, when she left her birthplace of London, England, and moved to Guyana, South America. She then moved to the United States as a young teen.

Michelle was nominated for the 2003 Emma Award for Favorite New Author, and continues to write romances with complex characters and intricate plots. Visit her Web site for further information at www.michellemonkou.com or contact her at michellemonkou@comcast.net.

# Trail of Kisses

THE LADIES *of* DISTINCTION

## Michelle Monkou

KIMANI™
ROMANCE

In memory of M. J.—Gone too soon.

KIMANI PRESS™

ISBN-13: 978-0-373-86151-4

Recycling programs
for this product may
not exist in your area.

TRAIL OF KISSES

www.kimanipress.com

**Printed in U.S.A.**

Dear Reader,

Asia Crawford may have had a few hard knocks in life. Trace Gunthrey may have suffered tremendous loss. Yet they can celebrate life's blessings through their deep friendship. Take the time to celebrate *your* friends and what you bring to each other's lives. Friendships are priceless.

As a member of Sigma Gamma Rho Sorority, Inc., I wanted to create stories highlighting the tight bond among sorority sisters. African American fraternal organizations have had a long history of servicing our communities, forming powerful networks and working with our youth.

If you are a member of a sorority or enjoy a close-knit group of dear friends, please share your positive experiences in building on sisterhood beyond the family. I have great friends now and from my past, and I look forward to forging more friendships in the future.

Contact me at michellemonkou@comcast.net.

Stay tuned for Naomi's story, which will bring the LADIES OF DISTINCTION miniseries to a close.

Blessings,

Michelle Monkou

# Chapter 1

"I understand the purpose of Operation Oasis in Colorado, no less." Asia Crawford lifted a devilish red lacy thong with the crook of her pinky finger. She eyed the offending object with a raised eyebrow. "What I don't understand is why I'll need this—or any of those." Her gaze shifted to the gifts of books and candy, before she jutted her chin toward the tiny mound of square latex packages.

"I provided the books," Denise remarked. "I don't know what your other sorority sisters have in mind." She wrinkled her nose with distaste.

"Actually I've come to expect this of you, Denise. You've made my birthday parties quite the talk." Asia surveyed the pile of sex accessories. "I'm not sure about what's the connection between getting laid off and getting laid?"

"Sex soothes the soul." Naomi folded her long, athletic body onto the sofa next to her. "Plus, it's been a year since you've been with a man. Although I don't consider Jack to be a real man. So you've had what is called a dry spell. Not good for maintaining positive karma."

"Well, being summoned in the middle of the day at work to Human Resources with an escort, and told that I have to exit the premises immediately, doesn't make me want to have sex." Asia remembered spending the first hour in a fog unable to grasp reality as she'd driven home. When the fog lifted, the full impact threw her emotions into a tailspin. She'd cried, railed at the unfairness and lain in bed staring at the TV into the weekend.

Despite her rationale that her dismissal was purely a business decision, the creeping sense of failure ate at her fragile confidence. Her life appeared to be crumbling like dominoes, as one thing crashed into the other until she lay flat, almost lifeless. Everyone told her that another door of opportunity would open. The thought was sadly comedic. In this economy, she'd have to open the doors, along with the windows.

"Here's a cosmo."

Asia took the drink from Sara. She prepared herself for a lecture, as Sara was known for delivering.

"I know you can't completely put this nasty business out of your mind. But today this intervention has one purpose—a much needed trip to get away from Chicago for a while."

"An intervention?" Asia almost choked on the heavy serving of vodka laced with a hint of cranberry. She had to thump her chest until the hit of alcohol faded. "I don't have any addictions, other than T.G.I. Friday's Brownie Obsession. Not sure what you've heard, although, thanks for all this…I think."

"I'll leave that comment alone. Now, getting back to the matter at hand, Operation Oasis is more than sexy underwear and physical gratification. You've always been there for each of our trials and been there for the celebrations. Let me remind you that the undergrad sorors presented you with the mentorship award for reaching back to pull up your sisters and for serving as a role model. You've done so much for so many. The least we could do is to provide a retreat of sorts with this spring trip to Colorado." Sara's presentation struck a humorous note with Naomi, who snorted. Asia bit her cheek to keep from giggling. "You need some spark back in your life," Sara added, waving off their silly behavior.

"And heck, it can't hurt to jump on a harmless booty call with a sexy, consenting hunk," Naomi added, banging her fist into her open palm.

Asia shook her head, making a face at Naomi's skewed philosophy of life and the role of sex. She shoved the lacy undergarments back into the gift bag. Her sorority sisters meant well when they planned and executed rescue missions. After all, she had participated in, and even led, several. Being on the receiving end was beyond embarrassing, though. All playing aside, her sorors' love threatened to start her tears. And she'd cried enough.

"This is supposed to be a good thing, Asia." Naomi threw her arm around her. "I thought that you'd cheer up."

"Sorry. I'm touched. Y'all are too much… Thank you." This time the tears surfaced. "This is a bit like winning the lottery."

"Yep, an all-expenses-paid getaway in the beautiful springtime Rockies, with a couple of Benjamins thrown in, and the possible bonus of getting picked up by an old rich man." Naomi nudged her in the ribs. "See if he's got a friend."

"Or being picked up by a fashion model on vacation. Good-looking, sexy, confident." Sara sighed with a dreamy expression.

"Hmmm...or a gorgeous bad boy running from the law." Denise did a little dance shuffle.

"Er...that's not going to happen," Asia answered. "None of those other fantasies, either. I plan on catching up on sleep, reading and updating my résumé. I may even go back to college. I'm using this time to kick my butt in gear and get focused. I have bills to pay. No way, no how, am I moving home with my parents." Asia shook her head for reiteration.

Naomi sighed. "You're hopelessly boring at twenty-nine. As the saying goes, Asia, 'Never say never.' Let me get you to the airport and send you on your merry way."

"But let us know how things are going. I wanted to come on the trip, but Naomi wouldn't let me. She thinks that you needed a solitary retreat," Sara added, pouting.

"I'll call, text, tweet." In reality, Asia welcomed the solitude. Having a twin made that goal difficult to attain sometimes.

She used to enjoy the attention, as a child, whenever she and Athena, her identical twin, were together. Dressing alike wasn't distasteful until high school, when she liked the same guy as Athena. When he obviously didn't bother noting the differences between them and crowed about dating twins, she and Athena dumped him, then decided to find their own styles.

Athena took the more brash approach to life, with lots of drama, at least one grounding a month and trips to their grandmother for stern lectures. Asia stayed on the sidelines as a spectator, seeing the distress and disappointment from her parents. Although she envied Athena's zany attitude, she quelled her impulses and worked on pleasing her parents and, in particular, her grandmother.

Now, her sister pursued her dream as a teacher on the small Caribbean island of La Isla del Azur. More importantly, she'd found her soul mate, Collin, and was head over heels in love.

The wild streak in her nature had taken a turn toward calm self-assuredness. Asia wondered if her sister could still understand the tumultuous feelings of discontent. Thank goodness she also had the strong relationships with her sorority sisters.

Naomi clapped her hands. "Party over, my ladies of distinction. Got to get Asia out of here on time. Take whatever food you'd like. Since Asia will be gone for a few weeks, no leftovers allowed."

Asia took the cue to retrieve her suitcases from the bedroom. Naomi had given her a hint about the trip earlier that week with the statement that she stop focusing on pleasing everyone but herself. And her friend had relayed her observations, in excruciating detail, of how Asia had dumbed down who she was to maintain the facade of the perfect life with Jack, her former boyfriend; and how she'd stayed on the same career track in the health field to impress her parents, as Athena had found true happiness.

Naomi, as did the rest of her line sisters, knew her dreams, those that may be far-fetched, along with those tiny wishes that required little of her but to accept willingly. Her candor sealed the decision for Asia. Only then did she pack, because doing so with a time crunch would've made her more frazzled than she already felt.

A knock on the bedroom door interrupted her progress.

"Come in." Asia paused over her makeup bag. "Oh, hey, Sara, what's up?"

"Everyone is diving in to the food. Wanted to take a few minutes to chat with you."

"All right. What's up?" Asia continued tossing in a few last-minute toiletries.

"Nothing." Sara walked over to the edge of the bed and sat. Then she took a deep breath.

"Okay, now you've got me worried. Is something wrong?" Asia set down the bag and joined Sara.

"Gosh, no. This is about you, more than about me." She reached out her hand until Asia felt compelled to take it. "You've been keeping to yourself lately. I'm worried that it's more than being laid off. I'm worried that you're still feeling blue over that jerk."

"You mean Jack?"

"Jack, the jerk…yes, him."

"You don't hold back." Asia liked her privacy, including her personal business. Most times her sorors accepted her quirks. But Sara wasn't one to follow rules. "Jack messed with my head, more than my heart. I'm not brooding about it. But I'd be lying if I said that I plan to go down that romance road anytime soon. My heart has a Do Not Enter sign at the moment."

"Learning a lesson is always a good thing. But you know what I'm going to say."

"That I can't paint all men with the same brush." Asia held up her hand. "I appreciate your words of wisdom but you're the ultimate romantic."

"Don't brush me off. You plan out everything in your life. Success is your middle name. You expect high results and, for the most part, it comes your way. I know that you expected a long relationship with Jack, maybe even ending up in a wedding."

Asia shrugged. Her sorors always did like to psychoanalyze. But she wasn't the type to pull up a chair and share.

No one knew how hurt she was after Jack accused of her not letting him be "the man" in the relationship. The women in her family prided themselves on being strong and in charge of their destinies. She didn't set out to be anything less than that.

Her style intimidated him. So without any warning, he'd rejected her. Their plans to marry, have a family and grow old together were destroyed. He wanted a woman who needed him. Whatever that meant.

She wanted his friendship, commitment, respect. She would've told the whole world, including her sorors, that they had those things between them. Reality forced her to be honest—she saw all of Jack's failures from the beginning. Trying to change him was a futile exercise. Not once did she miss him after they went their separate ways. Her ego, more than her heart, suffered the bruising. However, she didn't plan to repeat the same mistakes or go down the same path.

"Promise you'll get your head together and not dwell on what could have been." Sara reached into her pocketbook and tossed out an additional box of latex protection. "These are highly recommended. A couple of weeks to let the freaky side of Asia emerge. That jerk tried to destroy who you are. The job used your talents and then discarded you. Time for you to relax and do a whole lot of releasing. I know you have it in you. College days weren't so long ago." Sara grinned with too much mischief.

Asia looked down at the box in her hand. One more thing to add to the makeup bag.

"Hurry up, Asia. We need to get on the road." Naomi popped her head into the room.

"Don't overthink. Go. Live life a little. Get your mojo back." Sara kissed her cheek and left the room.

Asia looked around the bedroom. Everything was neatly in its place, thanks to the Container Store. Her life used to fit in neat cubbyholes. Organization, planning ahead and setting goals gave her comfort. She pulled up the handles of her suitcases and yanked them behind her.

She stepped into the living room. "I'm ready."

"Have a blast!" Denise hugged her.

"If you're having too much of a good time, call me. I'll be there in a jiffy." Sara added her hug.

And with a boisterous send-off, Asia accepted her sorors' farewell. Minutes later she headed to the airport for her attitude intervention program in the Rocky Mountains—specifically, Brewers Ridge, Colorado.


Asia walked the path leading to the house. Naomi had promised her a nice rustic vacation spot in the mountains, but the building in front of her wasn't exactly an old-fashioned log cabin. This house, built of massive logs, belonged in a high-end architectural magazine. It was three stories high and separated from any neighbors by lots of surrounding land. For a few weeks, she would have full access to this luxury vacation home. Her line sisters could definitely use this for a girls' retreat.

"Naomi, you sure know how to hook up a sister," Asia mumbled as she pressed the doorbell.

"May I help you?" A middle-aged woman smartly dressed in a tailored pantsuit stood in the doorway. An assessment was made of Asia, with a lingering measured look at the slightly tattered sneakers she wore.

"I'm Asia Crawford. I think you were expecting me."

"Yes." A small frown worked across the woman's head. "Let me see. There you are. For one second, I thought maybe my associate misplaced your reservation. She is new, you see, and still a bit unsure of herself. By the way, I'm Veronica McBeal." She stepped back for Asia to enter. "Did you have any problems with your flight or driver?" Confirmed as a client, Asia now received a warmer reception.

"Nope. As a matter of fact, it was one of the best trips I've had." Flying first class did make a difference—leg room, fine food and passengers of the upper income persuasion.

"Great. Let me give you a tour and then I'll turn over the keys. We have the credit card information already, so we are all set on the little details."

"Thanks." Asia didn't want to know how much this place must cost. Even if she'd planned to use her credit card, she didn't think the limit would've been enough to cover a couple of nights, much less a few weeks.

The rental associate dutifully led her through each level. Her polished presentation reflected excitement as they toured the bedrooms, and then checked out the various amenities, such as the oversize tub with jet propulsion openings. Quite clearly the bathroom facilities held a very personal charm over the woman. Asia planned to discover if her hype was true that night.

"You must have a waiting list for this place." Asia held on to the key with both hands.

"Yes, we always do. The location allows for privacy, but it's close enough to the resorts for ski enthusiasts in the winter. Spring is a perfect time to walk along the hiking trails. We've got a security detail overseeing the property, so you don't have to worry."

Asia nodded. Having a millionaire assaulted or kidnapped would ruin business. Even though she wasn't anywhere near that income bracket, she would have fun playing with the fantasy. Already the urge to relax and let loose stirred in her. An all-expenses vacation tended to have that effect. Too bad she didn't know a soul and didn't plan on making friends.

"There's a shopping mall twenty miles north. All the major stores, movie theaters and restaurants are there. There's even a year-round skating rink. You'll have fun." The rental associate looked down at Asia's luggage. "Is anyone else coming?"

Asia shook her head. "The suitcases are all mine."

"Good. We do have some wealthy eligible bachelors that make this their top vacation spot." Veronica winked. "Maybe you'll get lucky."

Maybe she had "starved for sex" on her forehead. She sighed. Even in her wild days, she sought a relationship; one-night stands, or two-week stands, didn't appeal to her. She believed no man had the kind of chemistry to upturn her world.

"All righty now, I'm going to get out of your hair. If you need anything, doesn't matter what time of the day, give me a buzz."

"Thank you." Asia tucked the business card in her pocket. She had no intention of calling Veronica McBeal. Since mentioning that she was alone, the eager light in the woman's eyes made her want to run far away. She wasn't looking for a buddy or matchmaker.

Once the lady left, Asia locked the door, then leaned her head against it. One year after being dumped, two weeks after being laid off, she was in Colorado vacationing in a luxurious home. So why not enjoy every minute, every inch of this treat.

Every day she unwound slowly, taking her time to settle in to her new surroundings. A week later, in the middle of unpacking her luggage, she had the urge to listen to music… and as loud as possible. She pulled out her iPod and inserted it into the docking unit. What better way to test the system? She turned the volume dial past the halfway mark. The hip-hop tune pulsated around the room, its heavy beat inviting her to dance with wild abandon.

And Asia danced, not caring that her steps were a bit dated. The freedom of shaking her hips without inhibition raised her spirits. She twirled around the room, using the free space as her *Soul Train* line.

When she grew tired of her dance-a-thon, she kicked off her sneakers, then her socks. With no roommates, she didn't have to worry about being neat. That's what this vacation was for. She went to the bathroom and turned on the faucet of the tub.

She shimmied out of her shorts and let them fall to the floor in her bedroom. Within seconds, she stripped down, headed to the bathroom and stepped into the water. She moaned as her body submerged under the warm water. The music selection had now shifted to R&B, a perfect complement. Asia closed her eyes to enjoy the soothing effects of the water. The music, with its haunting melody, relaxed her mind, erasing the worrisome fears, bit by bit.

As he pumped gas, Trace Gunthrey watched his twelve-year-old daughter bop her head to the music she piped directly into her ears with tiny earphones. He enjoyed the brief respite outside the SUV and away from Hannah's open hostility and cynicism. His patience wore to the thinness of paper, dealing with her attitude in the vehicle's confines. This same ugly disposition launched a series of consequences for her that now included a mandatory time-out in Brewers Ridge, Colorado.

Hannah, his little girl, was an only child. He noted that, from the type of clothing she often wore, his little girl was fading fast. A physically mature young woman now stood poised to emerge, demanding her place on life's stage. Often labeled as the invader, Trace had received many angst-filled rants. His battle between playing cop and indulging his guilty conscience by giving in to her demands left him confused and frustrated.

Trace took a deep fortifying breath as he replaced the

gas pump and took his receipt. He walked to her window and tapped on the glass. Hannah's instant glare screamed its message, then she cut her eyes away from him with disdainful dismissal. Patiently, he waited until she slid down the window.

"Do you want a soda?" Trace asked.

Hannah shook her head.

"You can speak," he scolded. Holding back the lecture, he continued, "How about food?"

"No."

"You need to eat. Drinking that potent caffeine drink isn't sufficient or healthy."

"Don't want anything from that shop." Hannah wrinkled her nose, as if an unpleasant scent oozed from the place. "The food's probably stale."

"We can stop at one of the restaurants right off the next highway." Her eyes narrowed, a sign of her customary readiness to reject anything he suggested. "Besides, I could do with a recharge. We've got three more hours. The last stretch can be the hardest."

"Fine."

Trace entered the SUV and aimed it west on Interstate 70. Her silent acquiescence allowed him one small, if brief, victory. Hannah's mood was too volatile and unpredictable to think that this wasn't just a temporary reprieve.

Harsh bass beats of a hip-hop song poured from her earphones. How many times had he warned her about listening to her music at such a high volume? Knowing Hannah, she'd take great pleasure in deliberately irritating him by rebelling against the smallest rule. Thank goodness the next exit was only a quarter of a mile. His foot eased down on the accelerator.

From the deep orange sky, he expected the sun to set in

another hour. Looked like he'd have to find their destination in the dark. Soon Trace pulled up to a restaurant that advertised home-cooked meals. His mouth watered at the thought of a hot meal that his mind conjured. Like the call of the wild, his stomach responded with a series of deep rumbles. He followed Hannah into the building and hoped that the wait wouldn't be too long. A small crowd already waited in the lobby. *Great.* At least Hannah didn't seem to mind. She continued to bob her head to the mystery beat.

Before too long, they were led to a table in the middle of the bustling dining area. Trace didn't mind the location. Hannah, however, shaped her mouth into her classical pout.

"We'll be fine," he reassured the waitress, who also noticed Hannah's displeasure. "Thanks." He took the menus, handing one over to his daughter.

Trace reviewed the menu. Tired and hungry, he opted for a steak dinner. "Are you ready to order?"

"Yes, Dad."

Trace hoped his face didn't reflect his surprise at the polite, quiet tone. He signaled the harried waitress that they were ready. The woman, who looked worn around the edges, took his order.

"I'll have the crab-artichoke dip, the fried chicken special and the chocolate cake." Hannah looked up at him. "I'll also have the old-fashioned, thick vanilla milk shake."

"No problem, little lady. You've got a big appetite for that tiny body." The waitress looked up from the order pad and smiled at Trace. "I've got two boys myself. Boy, can they eat."

"I hope you don't think you were being cute to get my father to give you a big tip."

The woman's face flushed a tomato-red, offsetting the loose copper-red ponytail. Her heavily colored lips worked in feverish embarrassment. Her gaze shifted between her two patrons.

"Please excuse my daughter's rude behavior." Trace stared at the rebellious eyes glaring back at him. "It's that behavior that earned you a suspension." Trace ordered his food.

"You can go now." Hannah flicked her hand at the waitress when she knew her father had finished. The woman glanced at him with a look that hovered between astonishment and bewilderment. No need to interpret. Her expression labeled him a wimp.

"Young lady, what do you hope to prove with your attitude? I'm not sure you realize that there are consequences for your behavior. Like what you're going through now, for example. First you vandalized the school. Then you cursed the principal. I still can't wrap my mind around the fact that you would take on school security. The only thing holding them from taking more punitive measures is your school record and the stellar student you once were." He held her hand in a firm grip before leaning over the table. "You can't stay angry at the world." How long should he give her a pass, knowing that her behavior stemmed from the loss of her mother?

"Yes, I do know the consequences—a boring lecture."

"That's enough!" Trace banged his hand on the table. His patience snapped from his control like a string popped from a balloon.

The other patrons shifted their attention toward him. Burdened by his anger and general frustration, he didn't care what they thought. He only focused on his daughter.

Hannah was the image of her mother—eyebrows that arched high over round eyes, a small rounded nose and soft round cheeks framed by thick, unruly dark brown hair. The one distinctive attribute she got from him was the amber-green hue of her eyes.

Those accusing eyes blamed him for her mother's death two years ago, as if he should've recognized the colon cancer symptoms earlier and forced her mother to see a doctor. At first he and his daughter had formed a unit bonded by their shared devastation. They'd grieved, especially at home, where all the memories were vivid.

During that time, he'd turned back to his work as a judge in the juvenile system, while Hannah had turned to after-school sports. Or so he'd thought. Maybe he was too eager to believe that she'd moved on and was capable of handling the overwhelming emotions.

Without warning, her feelings hardened against him. He reached again for his diminishing reservoir of patience. How he wished that he had the perfect solution.

Trace offered a half smile of apology to those sitting closer to him. "Time's up. This meal is over."

"But we haven't even gotten our food yet," Hannah whined.

"You can have it to go." Trace looked at his watch, mentally adjusting the delay on the trip.

"You said we can stop for dinner." Hannah raised her voice. "Dinner isn't even started."

"Here are your options." Trace stood and walked around to Hannah's chair. "You can get into the car with the food or you can get into the car without the food. But I've had enough. It's in your best interest to heed me." He used every power of mental telepathy to add emphasis to his statement.

"Fine." Hannah stood and followed her dad as he got the food to go and paid the bill, leaving a healthy tip.

Within minutes Trace was back on the road, Hannah had inserted her earphones, ate her food, and silence reigned. Although he wasn't sleepy, he felt the tiny threads of exhaustion still tugging at him. He popped a mint into his mouth for the sugar rush and cool blast.

He could've flown. This torture would've been over in three hours. Instead, he'd wanted more time to engage Hannah in a discussion that may've revealed the reason for her frequent meltdowns. Unfortunately, his skills as a judge didn't seem to have any effect with Hannah. His attempts at psychoanalyzing her bounced off the invisible shield she erected around herself.

He thought of the advice he gave to beleaguered parents who came before his bench with their children. Now he stood in their shoes with the familiar weight of failure on his shoulders. He'd turned for help outside the family, which led him to this point. His stomach clenched over the stress of his decision. New Life-New Purpose Camp for Girls would have a new, but unwilling, recruit.

"This had better work." He hit the steering wheel with the heel of his hand. A quick glance to his right showed Hannah had fallen asleep. "Good." She didn't need to see his agony, his vulnerability.

In the darkness, he drove into the night, relying on the navigational system to show him the way. If only he'd such a device in his head to guide him down the right path. His wife used to be the one with all the answers for life's curveballs. She had the sensitivity that he lacked. He missed not having to feel so blind and disconnected. Now all that mattered was Hannah. He'd try any means to keep her feet on the right, solid path.

The monotone GPS voice announced that the car had made the turn onto Cascade Loop. Darkness enveloped the car, causing Trace to slow down. He didn't want to drag out the torture any more than necessary. From the street, he caught glimpses of lights among heavy tree coverage. House numbers were painted along the curb. He had to pass three more properties before he found his rental. Each property had to be several acres apart. Finally, he pulled into the driveway that curved and ran on for several feet before ending at a large log home. He noticed a few lights on in the house. *Probably on a timer.*

"Wake up, Hannah," Trace called out.

Hannah moaned and squirmed in her seat, but her eyes never opened.

Trace looked around the area. No sign of anyone, but that didn't mean anything. His instincts honed in for the slightest sign of a harmful encounter. He popped the trunk and got out of the car. While Hannah slept a little longer, he'd get the luggage to the door, at least. However, he still kept a wary eye on the surrounding darkness.

The night air had a noticeable chill. Trace zipped his windbreaker jacket to seal in his body's warmth. He checked on the state of Hannah's attire. Maybe her classic hoodies would come in handy in the mountains.

Soft music wafted from the house. He paused, a bit puzzled about the sound. Again he looked around, but didn't see any signs that anyone was around.

There was a garage, but he'd get the remote after he registered. He unlocked the door and pushed the luggage just inside the house. The rental company had boasted about its hospitality. So far, their reputation was intact, with lights, music and even a stocked bar for convenience.

Trace headed back to the car for Hannah, where he gripped her shoulder and firmly shook her awake. Her eyes flickered open, and in an instant the usual frown slid into place for his benefit.

"We're here. Let's go inside."

She stumbled against his arm as she sleepily wound her way into the house. Her legs moved only when he half dragged her every few feet alongside him. Several yawns and a full stretch brought her more awake once they were inside.

But Trace was no longer focused on his daughter. The dimmed lights in the living area didn't hide the shoes and socks that littered the floor. Wouldn't the rental company clean the property? He'd paid too much to tolerate such an oversight.

"Dad, where's my room?" Hannah had her luggage in hand.

"Upstairs… Wait!" Something seemed off. "Stay here. Let me go investigate."

"I'm tired," Hannah whined. She flopped onto the couch and promptly curled up.

Trace let her sleep, taking the opportunity to complete his inspection of the house. If he didn't know better, he'd think that someone was staying here. But he'd picked up the key from the rental office. No one mentioned any problems.

As quietly as possible, he mounted the stairs. In the hallway, he paused in front of the room that he assumed was the master bedroom. His hand hovered over the knob. Taking a deep breath, he turned it and walked in.

Other than the crack of light from a doorway off to the side, the room was cloaked in darkness. The narrow shaft of light didn't illuminate the entire room. Partial shadows crossed the floor and bed. Dark shapes littered the floor. He moved forward to take a closer look.

The first lump he nudged with his foot. When he picked it up, it appeared to be shorts. Cautious, he allowed the shorts to slide out of his fingers back to the floor. Curious, he lightened his step and slowly eased his way farther into the room. Again he picked up a second object—panties.

"What the heck?" He dropped the underwear. Something caught his attention, so he listened keenly.

He heard the soft whoosh of someone breathing. Someone was in the room. And if he'd bothered to focus earlier, he would've detected the soft floral scent.

Trace walked toward the bed. But after the pieces of clothing he'd discovered, he wasn't sure whether to continue. He didn't want to stumble on a naked body.

Did this person break in? Were they mentally unstable and decided to fall asleep? Besides, how did *Goldilocks* end? He should've paid attention. Maybe the childhood story was the precursor to slasher movie flicks. Readying his nerves for a confrontation, he reached for the light next to the bed.

Bright light spilled onto the trespasser. A woman. She lay partially covered among the large assortment of pillows. Her face was relaxed and peaceful as she slept. Trace resisted the urge to get into her face, knowing that he'd scare her if she awoke.

The long drive with Hannah had worn his nerves thin. Maybe his thinking wasn't clear. All he knew for sure was that he'd made a reservation for this house, and had picked up the key on the way to the property. He returned downstairs to make sure there were no other visitors, while Hannah continued to sleep on the couch. Satisfied, he continued his investigation, covering the remaining bedrooms and bathrooms. No further surprises popped out at him. Looked like his visitor flew solo for this unlikely adventure.

He returned to the room where she slept. "Ma'am, you need to wake up." He glanced over to the phone. Should he underscore his request with a call to the police? She may be a woman, but in his line of work, he'd seen a lot of people who didn't conform to society's stereotypes.

She stirred, but only to snuggle the pillow closer.

"Ma'am!" His hand hovered over her shoulder. Trace expected an ear-shattering scream when she realized that she wasn't alone. He wanted his bed and this stranger out. "Ma'am, wake up, now!" He shook her shoulder with the same intensity as he did with his daughter when she was in a dead sleep.

Her eyes opened with sleepy irritation and then confused fright. Her mouth formed a perfect oval, while her eyes scrunched closed tightly. A vein popped to the surface, snaking down the middle of her forehead.

Trace cringed, readying for the onslaught.

## Chapter 2

Asia fought the panic. Her self-defense class urged the use of surprise and then to run like heck.

She pulled the pillow from under her head and threw it with as much force as she could into the face of her attacker. Her leg shot out and scored a hit. The tall trespasser buckled with a painful grunt.

With a quick roll off the other side of the bed, she scooted past him. Only then did she scream, using muscles, lung capacity and sheer adrenaline to break his eardrum.

Asia bounded down the steps, skipping the last few steps to hasten the descent. Her attacker stumbled down the hallway, clearly recovered enough from her assault for a pursuit.

"Stay away from me!" Asia screamed. This time she had no intention of taking him on. The element of surprise no longer existed. She headed for the front door for a hasty exit.

"Dad! What's going on?"

Asia backed up, hitting the wall hard. A young girl sat

up on the couch, clutching a backpack. She stared…before screaming.

Asia screamed back.

"Enough!" her attacker shouted above the din.

Asia's scream died in her throat. The young girl also stopped her screams.

"Who are you?" Her attacker walked over to the young girl and pulled her protectively into his arms. His eyes narrowed into a suspicious squint.

"What do you mean 'who are you'? I live here." Asia studied the odd couple, refusing to lower her guard. She stood between the front door and the telephone. Either option had major disadvantages. Her chances of fighting off two attackers were slim. But she wasn't going down without a major butt-kicking. She positioned herself in fighting stance, although she kept her fisted hands lowered at her side.

"Is she the maid?" The young girl looked up at the man.

"I don't think so. But whoever she is, she's worn out her welcome." He leaned over to turn up the side table lights.

"She doesn't look homeless," the girl added.

"No. She doesn't, does she? That means nothing." The man folded his arms, his face still set with grim determination.

"Excuse me, I'm still here. And I think you're the ones that have worn out your welcome." Asia decided the front door presented the better solution to this problem, other than serving as an exit for her. She walked over and opened the door. "You leave now or I'll raise the dead with a scream." The rental office would get an earful from her later.

"Please, no more screaming. My eardrums haven't recovered. I've rented this place. What is your excuse for being on this property?" The man pulled out a folded paper from his jacket. He approached her slowly with the paper in his extended hand. "Take a look. Here's my letter of confirmation for the rental."

Asia stared in his face for the truth, but all she noticed were piercing green eyes—a peculiar green that was more olive in color and touched with amber highlights. They dazzled her with a hypnotic effect. His throat clearing snapped her attention back, away from his face. She reached for the offered letter. A scan of the letter's contents revealed the bad news.

She didn't need to have her confirmation letter in front of her to recognize the letterhead and similar language. Everything was identical, except for the addressee—Trace Gunthrey. She raised her head to look at Trace, now that she knew his name. Knowing his identity didn't reveal anything worthwhile. His expression didn't shift from one of suspicion. She refolded the paper, trying to buy time to think of her options, before handing it back to him.

"So, you see, *you* are trespassing."

Asia closed the front door, suddenly aware of the night chill on her bare legs. The long T-shirt only struck her at midthigh. At the height of the adrenaline rush through her system, her lack of clothing didn't reach the top of her priority list. Now she eased her way toward the stairway. Her face flushed at being the underdressed one among them.

"She hasn't said who she is," the young girl persisted.

"I'm Asia Crawford." Asia's voice cracked under the stress. "My information is upstairs in the room, but I'd like to get dressed." She finished the request quietly, hating the helplessness that this situation created.

"We, my daughter, Hannah, and I, will wait here."

Asia backed away until her feet touched the first step, then she turned and hurried up the stairs, keeping a firm grip on the hem of her T-shirt. Trace may not trust her, but he had no problem looking at her legs.

* * *

Trace tried not to look at the long brown legs making a fast exit up the stairs. The exhaustion that had haunted him bade a hasty retreat. What he now felt came close to the aftereffects of an electric shock to the system. Thanks to Asia Crawford.

"Dad, don't you think we should call the police?"

"No, I don't think that'll be necessary." He gave his daughter a reassuring hug. "This lady seems to be okay. Unfortunately, I think we're about to learn that the place has been double-booked."

"Then maybe that's a sign that I don't need to be shuttled away to some camp for delinquents."

Trace chuckled. "Nice try. This situation will not affect you."

Then the woman appeared again at the top of the stairs. He watched her descend. The legs were covered in baggy sweat pants. Pity.

"Here's *my* confirmation letter." She extended hers with a triumphant smile.

Trace quickly surveyed it. He nodded. "Looks like we need to call the office." He walked over to the phone, taking charge of the moment.

"Can we do it in the morning?" Hannah complained. "Since we both are here, it's too late to go anywhere else. Besides, you said that she was okay."

Trace ignored Hannah's whine, along with her loose lips. Thankfully, someone picked up the phone. He turned his back to conduct the conversation.

"I'm Asia." Asia waved at Hannah, sensing that if she extended her hand, the gesture would be ignored.

"Hannah," his daughter answered. Her hands remained tucked in the front pockets of her hoodie.

"Would you like something to drink? I have milk or soda."

"Water is fine."

"Sure. I'll get it." Asia headed for the kitchen.

"I'm coming, too. My dad's conversation doesn't sound as if it's going okay."

"Sure." Asia looked back at Trace, who now paced with the phone wedged between his ear and shoulder. His hands punctuated his frustration, punching the air. What the heck was she going to do with her guests at two o'clock in the morning?

She poured a glass of water for Hannah, then decided that she might do well to hydrate. The man's voice had risen with a final punctuation of a growl.

He walked into the kitchen. "Looks like we need to hit the road, kiddo. In the morning, we'll get this cleared up. Quite clearly, the rental company made a mistake."

Asia saw Hannah's pout. However, she noticed weariness on the father's face, probably from the travel.

"I'm tired, Dad. Please, can't we just sleep on the couch until the morning?" Hannah turned her attention toward Asia.

"I'm not in the mood, Hannah."

"So, must we be punished for something that's not our fault?"

Asia shifted from one foot to the other. Why not be the Good Samaritan? Although they looked like nothing more than a single parent and his child, she didn't know these people, maybe they were fugitives. The girl was cute, but very cranky. And the exhausted dad was—in no plainer term—majorly fine. He had an understated, casual kick-butt sexiness. How could she not be hospitable?

"Look, why don't you stay here?" Asia offered. "There

are the two bedrooms down the hall that you're welcome to use."

Trace shook his head. "Thanks, but I think it's best if we leave."

"Best? We'll be in a cramped hotel. And she'll be in this big house by herself," Hannah accused, motioning to Asia like she was the culprit.

"Look, both rooms have clean linens and are very comfortable." Asia wasn't sure if she was being slammed in Hannah's analysis of the solution. But she wasn't having it. When the indecision still circled over Trace, she added, "And it's getting late. With the spring break season, the hotels are sure to be booked."

"Okay," Trace conceded. "Hannah, you can take the room up there. I'll stay in the housekeeping quarters. No one else is here, right?"

Asia shook her head. Good. Things were settled. She wanted to tweet to the world that a smooth chocolate, green-eyed hunk of a man would be sleeping a mere few feet from her.

As Trace carried the suitcases, Asia focused on assisting Hannah with her room. The girl easily dismissed her after the task was completed with placement of her earphones. Asia wondered if Hannah's attitude was due to her weariness, or if it was permanent. In the short time in her company, she'd reached her limit.

"Hannah, make yourself comfortable. Towels are on the shelves in the bathroom."

Hannah bopped her head and turned her back. Her body jerked to whatever beat pumped through her ears.

Asia stepped around Hannah until she stood face-to-face. "Would you like something to eat, maybe a sandwich?" When Hannah moved to repeat her dismissal of her, Asia placed a hand on her shoulder, halting her movement. She pulled out one of the earphones and stared unflinchingly into the girl's face. "Don't do that again. It's rude. You show me a little courtesy, and I'll return the gesture." Asia took a deep breath and backed up a step. "Let's start over, shall we?"

Hannah nodded, clearly stunned. "I'm not hungry…thank you."

"Well, then, have a good night." Asia smiled to ease the tension before closing the bedroom door. Outside of the room, she shook her head and chuckled. The girl was definitely a handful.

No wonder the father grumbled a lot. The girl's self-absorption would put anyone in a bad mood. Asia decided to go downstairs to check on his progress. He emerged from the room, before she knocked, and handed her several large bills.

"Oh, no, please don't do that. I'd consider it an insult to me." Asia stared at his hand, her frown deepening.

"Actually, I thought that I was being very thoughtful. You're paying to stay here. We'll only spend one night, but there's food and general inconvenience. I don't see why you should cover our stay."

"It's called hospitality. Allow me to extend it with no conditions. Hannah needs to rest. From the dark shadows under your eyes, I'd say the same rings true for you."

"Fair enough." His statement of acquiescence didn't match the unease that he radiated.

"Want to have a cup of coffee—decaf—before you hit the sack?" Asia wanted more time to learn about her guests. This big step—allowing a male stranger and his child to stay with her—did stir the doubts. She wasn't quite ready to close her eyes. Hopefully she could trust her instincts. "It won't take a minute to brew. Figure you may want to decompress after that phone call and the current state of affairs."

A few minutes later, the robust coffee scented the air with its intoxicating invitation. Asia set a steaming mug in front of Trace, and slid the sugar toward him. He shook his head, grasped the mug's handle and held the brew up to his nose, inhaling deeply. A smile, genuine and appreciative, broke through.

Asia took in every motion he made. Long fingers with trimmed nails fastened around the mug. She noted the slight curve that lifted the right edge of his mouth when he blew away the wispy steam curling above the rim. He gazed back at her, catching her staring.

"I'm really sorry to barge in and interrupt your sleep in that manner."

"I must admit, it was a bit of a shock." She smiled to show no hard feelings. "I'm glad that Hannah got to settle down."

He nodded. "She can be a handful when she doesn't get her way."

Asia sipped, biting down on the need to ask the probing question that stoked her curiosity.

"My wife—her mother—died two years ago." He cut off any further release of information by drinking from the mug.

"Very sorry to hear." She hadn't expected such sad news. "Hannah isn't taking it well?" She hated stating what seemed to be obvious.

"She was fine at first, coming out of the grieving. But in the past few months…" Trace's voice drifted with a tired resignation.

"You know, I lost my grandmother almost a year ago," Asia volunteered. "She was a force who blazed a path for others in the teaching profession. But more than that, she was the matriarch in every sense of the word, with a strict moral code on behavior. Nevertheless, I could go to her with problems or the smallest accomplishment and she'd offer her shoulder or applause. I know we're talking about different ages. Recovering from the loss can be like scaling the Rockies. There's no rule on how long that should last."

Trace barely responded with a nod. "Sounds reasonable, except life does have rules. As a judge, I have to live by those rules or occasionally use my discretion to waive them. As a father, I feel powerless and I hate being the enemy." He rubbed at the fatigue on his face before draining his cup and setting it down on the counter.

"I'll take that." Asia took the cup. "I don't have any experience with kids, but I do remember how I saw the world at that age. Anyone in a position of authority earned my dislike—as much as I could muster without raising my mother's anger. I wanted people to know that I had important opinions and wanted to be included in family decisions. I see Hannah displaying the same attitude. I welcome the challenge."

She walked with Trace as far as the stairs, where their final paths diverged. Bidding each other good-night, she went up to her room. A glance down the hall didn't reveal any light from under the door where Hannah slept. Good. The girl needed a good few hours of sleep. Maybe resting would help her disposition.

She closed her door and locked it. Sharing coffee with Trace did provide some enlightenment, but she took the extra precaution. Waking up with him in her room had almost caused heart failure. She didn't need a repeat performance unless…she invited him into her room.

That was purely her hormones talking. The man had just talked about losing his wife. How could she start thinking about him standing over her in the bedroom? Well she knew how she could start, but it wasn't right.

She reached over and turned off the light. With a frustrated grunt, she punched at the pillow. Her sorority sisters would die if they knew she'd invited a man to stay with her. If her body wasn't succumbing to sleep, she'd text them with enticingly enhanced details. Chances are they'd think she was lying. Wild stories about male conquests were never a part of her experience.


Trace slept on and off. He didn't have to guess why he tossed and turned through the night. Strange bed. Strange house. Strange set of circumstances. A woman, not strange, but wildly intriguing.

He looked at the clock, doubting that his daughter was awake. The child had no discerning taste when it came to her sleep. If he'd allowed her to stay on the couch, she wouldn't have complained. Yet, he wanted to make sure that she wasn't wandering around the house.

After taking a quick shower and dressing, he emerged from the housekeeper's room. The sunshine lit the house's interior uninhibited by the large pane of glass windows. He squinted as he tentatively maneuvered until his eyes adjusted. No one was up. He headed for the kitchen.

He surveyed the refrigerator and was surprised at how well it was stocked. Clearly Asia had planned to be here for a while. He grabbed the eggs, turkey bacon and loaf of bread. In short order, he found the pan and dishes needed for his breakfast fare. Whipping up a meal was no big deal. He cooked often for Hannah, his only chance during the week to spend some time with his daughter.

"Mmm. That smells good."

"Good morning." Trace hid his surprise. He hadn't heard

Asia enter the kitchen. "Just a small token of my appreciation for your hospitality."

"You didn't have to." Asia moved closer to stand next to him. "Looks good, though. By the way, I woke up Hannah."

"Thanks. I'm surprised that you still have your head."

"Let's just say, it's not as if she showed gratitude toward my consideration that she may be starved."

They shared a laugh. Trace discovered one more thing that he liked about his hostess. Asia had breezed into the room with such an upbeat manner that he found himself easily drawn into a casual conversation.

Asia took three plates. "Here, let me help get the food on the table."

Trace accepted her assistance, enjoying her light, breezy outlook.

The doorbell rang. The sound surprised him.

"Who could that be?" Asia looked at him, but all he could do was shrug.

She hurried to the door. At the same time, Hannah came downstairs and followed her father's signal to join him in the kitchen. He remained in the hallway watching Asia greet a woman. Then the stranger breezed past Asia to stand in front of him with a slick, toothy smile.

"Mr. Gunthrey, I'm glad I caught you here. I'm Veronica McBeal." The rental associate looked uncomfortable.

"Let's have a seat." Asia ushered them into the living room.

Trace noted that Hannah remained focused on eating her breakfast. He turned his attention back to the rental associate, who traded chatter with Asia.

"I am truly sorry for the mix-up. I would love to offer you access to one of our other properties, but we don't have any vacancies this week."

Trace didn't like the news. He had one day before Hannah went off to camp.

"I promise that you'll be able to stay with us for free, at another time. I hate not being able to set things straight for my favorite judge."

"Right now I have to find accommodations while my daughter is at camp. Do you have any recommendations?"

"Unfortunately, everything in the area is booked because it's spring break and we have a spring concert tour, plus it's the season for hiking and enjoying the blossoms."

"I do not believe what I'm hearing." Trace made sure to emphasize each word, not bothering to hide his irritation.

Hannah entered the room. "Since you can't stick around, looks like I won't have to go to camp." She grinned.

Trace felt sandwiched between the unforeseen circumstances of the double booking and his daughter's giddy declaration that he wouldn't leave her there. All his organizing and planning didn't matter. He'd paid for the camp, taken a brief leave of absence and turned his focus on Hannah. Her school would only consider her case if she'd enrolled and successfully completed a program.

Otherwise, expulsion could be considered. He didn't want to lean on his credentials for a favor. Her current therapist had recommended an intensive crisis management course. Hannah needed it. Admittedly, he needed it, also. He wanted to have his daughter back. Right now, he paused, seconds away from his breaking point.

Asia tried not to stare at Trace. But his obvious distress left her wondering why this trip was important. His defeat showed with his bowed head. Even his shoulders drew down, and he shoved his hands deep into his pockets. His mouth set in a grim tightness, with only his jaw working under the tension. Asia suspected that there was more under the surface with father and daughter. And in the few instances that she witnessed, she guessed that the daughter gained the upper hand, more often than not.

"Trace, may I speak to you?" Asia motioned with her head for him to follow her into the tiny library. "Veronica, we'll be right back."

She didn't presume that he would follow, but she was grateful to hear his footsteps behind her. Walking down the hallway provided the precious seconds to wiggle out of any further crazy thoughts she felt compelled to act upon. But when she walked into the room and closed the door, she hadn't come up with anything that would dissuade her. The first time she offered to share the residence was due to her inclination to be charitable. Now, she had ulterior motives.

"Miss Crawford, before you say anything, I'll be out of your hair in a few minutes."

"I like to be called Asia." She raised her hand. "I am extending an invitation for you and Hannah to stay. There's more than enough room for all of us to be here. I also look forward to getting to know your daughter." *And you.*

"I appreciate your kindness. But I think it would be more appropriate for me to stay elsewhere. Remember Hannah is going to a camp. I'll be alone."

"Look, you stayed in the maid's quarters, which, from the size, could pass for a one-bedroom efficiency. We won't be in each other's way."

"Well, the location is convenient to the camp." He rubbed his forehead. "There are no vacancies for miles." He pinched the bridge of his nose. "And I can't leave Hannah here to return home."

Asia allowed him to mull over her offer with various

rationalizations. She preferred to keep her emotional seesaw on the matter to herself.

"If I stay, then I have to pay my portion of the bill."

"That's considerate of you, but unnecessary." She changed her mind. She had no intention of letting her sorority sisters know she'd invited a strange man to stay with her. They had no confidence in her ability to catch and snag a man, much less to play roommates. She'd be accused of being a liar. Then they'd descend on the log cabin in their off-the-chain frenzied behavior. "I didn't invite you because of the cost. I simply wanted to help your daughter."

"Still, you have extended a wonderful invitation. I'll take you up on your offer." He extended his hand, then pulled back just before her fingers made contact. "Are you really sure? I understand if your husband or boyfriend may take issue."

"You're a judge, correct?"

He nodded.

"You have to live at a higher moral code?"

Again, he nodded.

"Then I'll have to trust in you—and in me—that I've made the right decision. Deal?"

Asia extended her hand, this time pushing it into his space, forcing him to abandon whatever concerns he felt.

"Thank you, Asia." Trace smiled.

Oh, boy, the mouth on that man was gorgeous. A smile more than enhanced his face, pulling her to look at every handsome feature in front of her.

They reentered the living area to see Veronica captured under Hannah's attention. Asia hurried forward, although the conversation appeared to be one way, with Veronica actively listening.

Veronica's gaze shifted from Hannah to them once they entered. Asia wasn't sure if the accusatory glare was directed at her. She looked up at Trace, whose gaze narrowed, all attention on Hannah.

"Mr. Gunthrey, I want to make it perfectly clear that this is a retreat, where people spend a sizeable amount of money and have high expectations about others in the community." Gone was the sales pitch. Her voice chilled the atmosphere.

Trace said nothing, although his tense stance spoke volumes.

"Whatever do you mean?" Asia spoke, feeling compelled to step in.

"People like their privacy. They are coming to escape from the rat race of life. As a community, we protect this special paradise."

Asia nodded. She didn't miss the smug grin on Hannah's face. More appeared to be happening than she or Trace knew. Veronica's demeanor had turned frosty and unfriendly. Her sudden coolness, mixed with Hannah's defiant raise of her chin, didn't bode well for Trace.

She'd extended her hospitality for his daughter's sake. Well, she was about to overstep, but still considered the gesture for Hannah's sake.

Asia cleared her throat. "Veronica, I think the matter has been resolved."

Hannah's grin wavered.

"Trace will be staying here while Hannah goes off to camp."

Now the young girl looked on in horror.

"I'm afraid that can't be done. You're the only tenant registered for this property. In the contract you signed to reserve the property, there is a stipulation that prohibits what you suggest," Veronica clarified.

"But this is an unforeseen circumstance." Trace shook his head.

"I'm afraid it's nonnegotiable."

"The mistake was yours," Trace said in a calm, soft, but lethal tone.

The rental associate bristled. Her mouth pursed with frustration.

"Seems to me that since the Gunthrey family have gone to the expense and effort to get here, and find that their reservation was mishandled, the least you could do is be amenable to making his stay a bit more pleasant." Asia turned to Hannah. "And I'm sure that Hannah doesn't want to miss out on her planned activities."

Veronica flung up her hands with an exaggerated sigh. "Very well, this is most unusual. I don't have a spare set of keys with me."

From the finality of her statement, Asia surmised that Veronica wouldn't be back in any hurry with the extra set. But she didn't care, she'd work it out between her and Trace.

Veronica made quick work of letting Trace and Hannah know about the amenities. Her discomfort was readily apparent as she maneuvered her way around and away from them. Occasionally, she targeted Asia with her displeasure. Asia simply smiled just to annoy her. After Veronica left, the tension deflated and slipped from the room.

Asia turned to her two new guests. She offered a big smile with arms thrown wide in a hearty welcome to Hannah.

"I don't want to stay here," Hannah argued. "I don't want to go to any camp. You only want to dump me there like trash with all the other thugs and druggies!" Hannah's face pinched as her words shot out like targeted missiles at her father.

"Everything has consequences." Trace's anger added a rumbling bass to his voice.

Asia dropped her arms, swallowing her cheery welcome.

She wanted to leave the room, but it meant walking through the danger zone between father and daughter.

"Letting Mom die has consequences, too." Hannah turned and ran from the room.

Trace remained rooted, eerily still.

Asia opened her mouth, but any comforting words swirled in a jumble only to choke as she tried to respond. She heard a door slam down the hall. Hannah must have taken refuge in the bathroom.

She looked up at Trace, who hadn't moved, hadn't blinked, or said a word. Only a tiny visible pulse at his neck pumped.

In her family's circle, she avoided drama. But this family's hurt rose above the surface, with deep fissures and a rocky landscape ahead. She had a strong desire to jump in with a life preserver for Trace and Hannah. Neither one really wanted her assistance. If she could reach Hannah, she suspected that the weight pressing on Trace's shoulders would be lessened. Maybe she'd be showered by his distinctive smile a little more often. Whatever it would take, she wanted to help.

# Chapter 3

Trace counted to twenty yet his heartbeat didn't decelerate. Hannah's anger had struck him fast and with a ferocity that left stinging welts on his soul. He appreciated Asia's decision to simply leave him alone in the room. At this time, he couldn't accept any conciliatory gestures from her based solely on pity.

He pondered his next move. Should he give Hannah her space to bring her emotions in check?

His wife would've known how to deal with their daughter, whose teenage years blossomed exponentially with angst and extreme emotion. On the job, he'd lectured delinquents within an inch of their lives for less lip—but this was his daughter, who had a tongue laced with acid.

"Hannah." He tempered his tone, as he moved through the first floor looking for her. "Hannah, let's talk." He listened keenly for a sign.

A soft moan to his left caught his attention. He looked at

the closed door for a second, before his hand reached for the knob.

"Hannah, please open the door." He ran a hand over his head, praying that he'd pick the right thing to say. "Look, let's not fight. Honey?"

The door opened slowly, although with squeaky hinges. Staying even-keeled was normally his strong point, but in this instance, he wanted to break protocol and pull her into his arms. Unable to read what she needed from him, he didn't. He restrained himself to punctuate the serious nature of her actions. Lashing out at him with venomous rants couldn't become a habit.

Hannah, however, must have done some soul-searching. She looked up into his face. Tears streamed down her cheeks. Her hair, which had been in a neat ponytail, now framed her face in a disheveled crown. She stumbled into his body, wrapping her arms tightly around his waist. Her sobs muffled into his sweatshirt.

Just like that his resolve evaporated. He wrapped his arms around her and rested his chin on top of her head. Why couldn't it be like this all the time?

Trace cleared his throat. "You know we have to talk."

Hannah held on tighter.

He pried himself from her arms and raised her chin with the crook of his finger. "Have a seat."

They made their way to the nearby eating area off the kitchen. The four-setting dinette set was built for the traditional family to eat together. Sitting across from his daughter with no mom to fill the chair and no other sibling was the reality. She needed to understand that they had an unbroken bond.

"I didn't mean to say…" Hannah looked down at hands working nervously in a clenched entanglement with her fingers.

"I know." Trace didn't want to push the discussion about her mother. Instead, he focused on the purpose of the trip. "You can't go into the camp angry. It is a camp, not a jail." He leaned back, a bit worried that she had closed off listening to him. "I know the owners of this facility. They can help you. Hannah, you've got your whole future ahead of you. You're pretty, intelligent, full of energy. Don't waste it being so angry that you miss out on life."

"But I don't need to go to a camp for two weeks. I don't want someone telling me what to do from the time I wake up until I go to sleep. I promise that if you cancel this, I'll behave."

Trace shook his head.

"Please, Dad." She slammed her hands on the table. "I can't believe you won't put yourself in my place."

"You're a smart girl. Too smart for your own good because your mouth puts you in trouble. Now you have to obey someone else's rules. How about putting yourself in my position for a change?"

"Then I guess there's nothing further to discuss." Hannah pushed her chair away from the table.

"Stay put. We're going to continue this discussion. You're only in this house for one day before you leave for the camp. Let me warn you that you'll not disrespect Asia. You will assist with the dishes and mind your manners. Whatever game you pulled with the rental associate, you'd better not have a repeat performance." He stood, using his height and stern expression to cause her discomfort. "Do you understand?"

A brief glimmer of rebellion shone through the savage thrust of her chin. Trace didn't budge in his stance. His scrutiny didn't shift until she shifted her gaze and looked at her hands. She nodded.

"Shaking your head doesn't work for me."

"Yes," Hannah hissed. "I understand."

"Good. Now you can go."

He watched her slide out the chair. He wasn't so egotistical to think that her strong will had been broken. If anything, he could practically see the wheels of her brain grinding to come up with further options.

As Hannah headed for the stairs and probably her iPod, she passed Asia, who was headed his way. He wasn't really sure how to start the conversation with Asia, especially when he felt defensive toward any criticism. Maybe he could take Hannah's approach and pretend it didn't happen.

Asia didn't need subtitles to interpret Trace's body language. His embarrassment, as she approached, earned her sympathy for his discomfort.

"Coffee?" Asia moved toward the coffee brewer. "This time I think we should go for a full dose of caffeine."

"Sounds like what I need right about now."

His weariness poured out in his words. She hurried to make a fresh pot. "I hope you haven't changed your mind about staying here."

"No. Not all." He shifted his weight as he rested his hip against the counter. "Hannah will be leaving tomorrow."

"Oh. Guess that means you didn't change your mind." Asia didn't want her attempt at humor to overshadow the tension. "She's ready?"

The coffeemaker beeped, which pulled her attention from Trace. She pulled the mugs from the cabinet, then reached for the cream in the refrigerator. After snapping the door shut with her hip, she turned her attention to him.

"I don't need any sugar or cream." Trace reached for the oversize mug she proffered.

Asia waited to see if Trace would answer her question.

She couldn't pretend that she wasn't aware of the situation. And after all, he would be her roommate for two weeks. She sipped her coffee, trying to be patient.

"Do you have time for a quick tour of the mountain village?" She accepted his refusal to answer her previous question as the boundary that she couldn't cross.

"Sure. Let me get Hannah."

Asia continued sipping her coffee while he left the room. She noticed an odd occurrence whenever Trace left the room—it somehow felt empty. Granted, he was over six feet, but there was more to the phenomenon. Of course, maybe it was the attraction she felt toward him. Behaving like a girl with a high school crush freaked her out.

Later that day, Asia drove her guests down the narrow neighborhood road. No one spoke. Hannah stared out the window. Meanwhile Trace stared straight ahead.

Using her rearview mirror, she stole glances at the girl. She wished that she had more time to be around her to earn her trust. Their glances connected. Instead of a smile, Hannah shifted in her seat and turned her body toward the window even more.

"We can take a boat ride down the river."

"I don't like boats," Hannah flatly declared.

"Oh." Asia looked toward Trace for help. "There's a roller skating and Rollerblade park not far from here. Interested?" Asia again looked up at Hannah's reflection. She saw the glimmer of interest, that is, until Hannah looked back at her and squelched the desire with a sneer.

"Not interested."

Trace's head snapped to the left. "Mind your manners. Now, that's the last option or we can head back to the house."

"Fine. I'll go." Hannah muttered to herself in the backseat.

"Good, we'll go to the park, then swing past the old-fashioned ice-cream parlor." Asia tried to interject lightness in the close setting of the car.

"Oh, that would be—" Hannah began in a cartoonish voice.

"Swallow whatever you were about to say—for your own good." Trace unsnapped his seat belt and leaned between the two front seats.

Asia almost slammed on the brakes. She didn't know whether she'd have to save Trace's life, by pulling over, or his daughter's life, as her father only left a couple inches between their faces. Plus she didn't need a fat ticket by a vigilant cop.

"Yes, sir."

"Trace, I need you to put on your seat belt." Asia touched his arm to get his attention.

"Sorry about that." He slid in his seat and obeyed her request. "Consider the infraction a mission of mercy for all of us."

"We're almost there." Asia guaranteed her statement with a slight acceleration. They all needed to get out and walk off the anxiety. The constant battle of wills placed too much pressure on what should've been a final day to enjoy each other's company.

The Rollerblade park proved to be popular. The parking lot barely had any spaces left and Asia had to park in the overflow lot. The air was filled with screams, laughter and raucous noises from preteens to those who may have just crossed the legal age.

Hannah jumped out of the car. The swirl of activity

definitely caught her attention. She didn't pay any mind to Asia, who called her.

Asia tried again. "Hannah, let's go rent the board. You'll have to pick what you need." She bravely placed an arm around the young girl's shoulders. To Asia's delight, Hannah didn't shrug it off. "You know, I'm a bit envious that you can skateboard. I could barely roller-skate when I was your age."

"You should try," Hannah said, looking up her. "And I'm also good at photography."

Asia smiled. She wasn't sure if Hannah had raised a challenge. Trying to dare her wouldn't work because Asia knew and accepted her limitations. Falling on her behind for any period of time held no attraction.

"I'll help you. We'll be in the slowpoke lane." Trace grinned at her before stepping up in the line to order the necessary equipment.

Hannah was dressed with the requisite pads in minutes. She clutched her skateboard under her arm.

"You don't have to wait for me." Asia waved her on.

"We'll be in this section. Be careful," Trace shouted after his daughter's retreating figure.

Hannah maneuvered through the crowd on the skateboard like someone who had spent hours perfecting the art of balancing on a short piece of wood with wheels. In a matter of minutes, she had bonded with another girl who was equally tentative about joining the masses. They showed each other their skills, communicating with all manner of nonverbal cues, until a consensus had been reached. Hannah offered them a short wave before disappearing in the boisterous throng.

"That went well," Asia offered.

"Yes. Thank you," Trace said. "Here, have a seat." He guided her to a bench with barely enough room for one.

"Thanks for what?" She sat, then tried to inch over so he could also sit.

"Well, you knew what could bring Hannah out of her dumps. I appreciate everything you've done. Sometimes, it can all get a bit…"

She didn't need him to finish the sentence. Although she had never been in his place—being a sole provider or having someone dependent on her—she could be sensitive to the issues. In her opinion, he needed solid support to help him handle his daughter and to cut himself some slack when things didn't go the way he wanted.

"Let me have your right foot." Trace bent down on one knee with his hand outstretched. His eyes twinkled at her mortified expression.

"I really did mean it when I said that I can't skate. It wasn't for Hannah's benefit," she said.

Trace cupped her heel and rested her foot on his thigh. His fingers worked at her shoelaces, then slipped off her shoe. Asia tried to keep from wiggling her toes or erupting into a giggling mess.

"I find that people are afraid of things they don't understand. Or if they had a bad teacher, the experience ruined any future plans."

"Like my fear of math."

"Yep. And I'm a fantastic teacher for roller skates. Won a couple competitions, too."

"Means I'm in good company." She rested her booted foot on the ground and allowed him to tend to her left foot.

Every time he looked up at her, she practically had to hold on to the bench with both hands to keep from falling over. His gaze had a hypnotic gleam. Darn those gorgeous green eyes and thick black eyelashes.

Finally, the time came for her to stand and head toward

the rink. She managed to stay upright only because Trace had locked her into place beside him with his arm around her waist and his other hand caught in her tight grip. Her determination to keep her feet from rolling in opposite directions quelled her lighthearted attempts at a discussion.

"You can relax," Trace said near her ear. "I can feel your heart pounding away. Lean against me."

Asia didn't comply. She had to stay upright, on her own. His hands were merely support. Plus her disposition would improve if his body wasn't so firm against her.

"If you don't let me guide you, we'll both fall."

"Just let me hold on to the rail."

Trace's hands moved away from her, although he remained close. She screamed and clutched air before she had a handful of his shirt in her fist.

"Now will you let me lead?"

"Is this how you teach?" she asked, her chest heaving with the exertion. She didn't wait for his arm to encircle her waist before leaning into his side. "Even if I don't fall, I think that I'm going to feel muscles that I haven't used in a long time."

"Then we'll have to do this again. Only for your body's sake." He winked down at her.

After one lap around the rink, Asia allowed herself to relax a smidgen. Trace's body guided hers, his perfect form making long sweeping strokes that alternated with each leg. She raised her chin, enjoying the cooling effects of the spring day.

"I think that I'd better check on Hannah," Trace said, interrupting her thoughts. He guided her to the rail, then pulled out his phone. "Since she's not checking in with me, I better do it."

"Sure." Asia felt embarrassed that she hadn't suggested looking for Hannah. Instead, her mind had gone where it had no business going. The first man who was in her company for more than a few minutes, and she practically melted at the attention. "I'll try to do a lap on my own." She didn't wait for him to look up from texting.

Trace paused in typing his note to watch Asia's retreating figure. Her legs glided to the rhythm. She looked good coming or going.

He shifted his attention back to the phone and finished his text. As he waited, he scanned the crowd, looking for the bloodred jacket that Hannah loved to wear. Unfortunately there was nothing unique to that piece of clothing since many kids wore the same hoodie style.

A girl's squeal to his right set his teeth on edge. Laughter followed. He exhaled. His overprotective nature would have embarrassed him if he'd scaled the railing to rescue his daughter.

His phone buzzed: Message received.

Dad, I'm fine. Learned a new trick. Gotta go.

His fingers poised over the keyboard, ready to continue the conversation. He snapped the phone closed and tucked it into his jacket pocket. He'd give her another half hour before texting again. Otherwise, he'd be accused of messing with her vibe.

"Everything okay?" Asia landed hard against the railing near him.

"Sounds like Hannah's having a blast."

"Looks like you're not."

"Oh, no. I'm having fun." He smiled, hoping to erase the small frown that hovered. "Debating on whether I should respond to her text."

"You're afraid that she'll get irritated?"

He shrugged. "I'm jumping in with both feet." He knew that he sounded like a parent who didn't know if he wanted to be a father or a friend.

"That sounded ominous." Trace looked over at her. "Let's rest here for a second. I like skating to the mellow tones of the seventies."

"I agree. This fast-paced, bass-thumping music is a killer on the thighs."

"Let's get a soda." Trace offered his hand, which she easily grasped. They made their way through the rink and headed for the concession area. "My treat."

"I accept."

He ordered two sodas and a small basket of fries. He wanted a chance to get to know his new roommate. Two weeks could be short or could drag on for eternity.

"Time for the in-depth interview, huh?" Asia sipped her soda.

"We'll have to put the Q and A on the fast track. We're only a few hours away from our semipermanent deal." He watched her lips close over the straw. "Unless you've changed your mind."

"No. I'm too impressed with your credentials. Never met someone in the legal career tract, much less at your level. Just slightly intimidating."

"Don't worry, the clientele are generally around the sixteen-year-old category."

"That's tough. It's got to be a bit disappointing to see so many young people coming through the juvenile system. You're only seeing the bad, right?" Asia leaned closer to him, and her expression grew pensive.

"On the surface, it may seem that way. There are times when the court can provide the proper solution to a child's welfare, after the parents or legal guardians fail to live up to their responsibilities. But it's not so brutal and cold. The system isn't out to lock up and throw away the key to these children's lives."

"Are you a hard-nosed judge? Or are you moved by tears?"

Trace laughed. "Depends on the victim and the offender's attitude. Unfortunately at that age, it's easier to see the impact of upbringing on a child's life…" His voice drifted softly.

"Hannah will be fine," Asia offered. "I see a steely determination under the brashness."

"It's that brashness I'm afraid of. Otherwise, she might be standing before one of my colleagues if she doesn't get on the right path." Trace blew out a frustrated sigh. He rubbed his hands along his pants legs, as if to rid himself of the blues. "What about me, the person? Don't I impress you?"

Her examination covered his body to his face. He felt flushed, but refused to acknowledge that he could be blushing.

"Hmm. I like a man who isn't shy about getting compliments."

"Yep, I have no shame."

"Let's see." Asia tilted her head, pursing her lips into a playful pout. "I like the fact that you're caring, attentive and open to learning. I admire the depth of your concern for your daughter and determination to make things better. Some parents may have shipped her off to a relative, or turned to physical punishment out of general frustration."

"I hate not being able to soothe her pain."

"You've tried professional help?"

Trace nodded. He popped fries into his mouth in rapid succession. Eating was his way to soothe his pain. Then he worked out with a vengeance at the gym until he felt like puking.

"No change at all?"

"There are good days. She's coming out of her funk for longer periods, if that makes any sense. But then at the snap of a finger, she can muster up that deep-seated anger and turn it on anyone. That's what worries me—that there is some part of her that she has closed off even from the therapist."

"And this camp is going to help?"

"It has to. Earlier in the month, Hannah took on a group of girls, the bad-ass kind. She claims that they were picking on another girl, but the girl wouldn't corroborate her story." He paused. "Hannah threw the first punch." He sighed. "And there were more problems where she turned her rage on a teacher. Then we had destruction of property because she's hanging with the wrong crowd." He ticked off all the infractions on one hand. "The principal, fights with students, and on and on, one incident after another."

"She doesn't seem to want to go to the camp."

"It's a boot camp, of sorts. Set in the mountains, they have a small number of girls assigned to a counselor. They'll get the attention needed to redirect them onto the right path, along with building up self-esteem, instilling discipline and pushing good old-fashioned hard work with life skills. Of course, none of these things appeal to Hannah. In her perfect world, she'd rather not socialize with anyone. Maybe that's why she gets lost in her world of photography. It's the one thing that brings her joy."

"All she may need is some time with you. Only you."

"I've done that." Trace had worked through all of this. He'd come to some sort of understanding with himself. Asia's prodding was rearranging the covering he had slid over the entire situation.

They finished the fries as the conversation quieted. Trace's phone buzzed with an incoming message.

"It's Hannah." Trace answered her, directing her to where they sat. "She's ready to go."

"Good. I think my aching muscles have had enough, too."

"I had so much fun," Hannah said, bursting upon them. Her cheeks were tinged with a touch of pink. Her eyes sparkled. The grin she wore revealed the clear braces.

Trace felt the swell of emotion that his daughter was capable of being happy and contented.

"Ready for ice cream?" Asia asked. She patted her stomach. "I'm stuffed, so count me out. But I'd be happy to drive you to the shop."

"Definitely. I'm so hungry," Hannah announced.

By the time they arrived back at the house, fatigue had set in on each person. The exhaustion made them all cranky as they groaned and complained about various body parts. Trace knew he'd pay for the roller-skating with sore knees tomorrow. However, the pain was worth the contentment in Hannah's demeanor.

As he settled in for the night, he didn't look forward to tomorrow, when he'd have to take her to the camp. Maybe she'd come out a little wiser and more in control of her emotions. Maybe with the promised therapy sessions, she would erase the guilt that held his feet in cement. So much was chance, but he had a lot of hope and a shaky amount of faith.

Without further prompting, he offered up a prayer. He asked for protection for his daughter, wisdom to know what to do and gratitude for a woman who had a generous spirit.

Asia closed the book of motivational experiences from various celebrities and tucked it into the nightstand. She snuggled down under the covers, plumped the pillow under her head and waited for sleep to come.

Sleep took its sweet time arriving. Maybe her thoughts were too much and too heavy for her to plunge into slumber land. Every minute that she spent with the Gunthreys, they had made an indelible impression on her. Too bad they would go back to their own world after this brief encounter, despite possibly promising to keep in touch. Asia had managed to have several short conversations, but she didn't think that she'd made any significant headway with Hannah. Asia saw that Hannah carried her sadness like a heavy, well-worn cloak.

She sighed and rolled over to wait for sleep. She had her own reasons that she wanted to help Hannah. The truth was she didn't believe that a two-week stint in a camp was the answer. In the brief time she spent with Hannah, she could tell the girl was not a delinquent. Hannah cared more than she pretended. She particularly cared what her father thought.

Asia rose onto her elbow and turned over the pillow to the cool side. Trace practiced tough love, but today she saw a softer side when he forgot to be preoccupied with worrying about his daughter. She enjoyed his deep rumbling laughter, his piercing gaze and the sinewy muscles of his embrace while they skated.

Asia wrapped her arms around herself. How would she ever be able to deal with Trace in this house? He was so tempting—and she wasn't feeling particularly strong.

Within eight hours, Trace would take Hannah to camp. Then she'd be here all alone with him. She bit her bottom lip, her thoughts racing toward sensual temptation.

Finally she closed her eyes. Sleep still eluded her. However, she gave free rein to her imagination to play out a very sensual game of what-if.

# Chapter 4

"Hannah, let's go." Trace stood in the doorway to her room. "I have your suitcase already in the car. I just need your body in the car."

Asia approached him with her hands open in appeal. He frowned at her, wondering if she was coming to Hannah's defense again.

"She's getting her stuff together," Asia explained. "Cut her some slack."

Trace paused. Asia's concern touched him, but also distracted him. It seemed she cared as much as he did about Hannah's happiness.

"You know, she can stay here…instead of going away." Asia didn't quite meet his gaze. She fidgeted, scratching her eyebrow.

"I appreciate your offer, but I'll pass."

"It's more than an offer. I think it's something that Hannah would appreciate."

"How do you know what she'd appreciate?" He smacked his forehead as soon as the words came out. "I'm sorry. Didn't mean to sound churlish."

"I didn't mean to sound as if I knew anything. She looks sad, that's all."

"After each infraction, she has a really good sad expression. Kind of like a pro. The other day she cried buckets of tears after that horrendous accusation. Then minutes later, the snark was back."

"Still…"

Hannah appeared with her backpack. "Ready."

"Wait a sec, I have something for you." Asia handed over a gift-wrapped box. "To remind you that I'm thinking about you."

"Can I open it now?" Hannah's voice carried her amazement.

"Sure."

Asia's assent was barely uttered before Hannah pulled the thin decorative ribbon. Her fingers removed the satin blue wrapping paper in seconds. Then she pulled off the top of the small box.

Hannah looked up at her. She had tears shimmering on the edges of her eyes. "Thank you," she whispered.

"It'll provide you with comfort."

Hannah pulled out the delicate gold necklace with a cross pendant. She placed it lightly along her palm and extended her hand for Trace to see.

He stroked her head, also touched by Asia's thoughtful gesture. Though their time together had been a matter of days, he couldn't quell the feelings she stirred in him. Her beauty attracted him, but her inner sensitivity and strength excited optimism like a blast of fresh air.

He waited for Asia to place the necklace around his daughter's neck. "Go ahead to the car." Trace stepped aside.

Hannah reached the doorway, but then turned and ran toward Asia. She wrapped her arms around Asia's waist, burying her head against Asia's chest. "I'm only going if Asia goes with us."

"Don't be difficult, Hannah."

"I'm not moving unless she comes." Hannah looked away from Trace and up at Asia's face. "Please."

Asia rested her hands on the child's narrow shoulders. She had her objections to this camp, but didn't want to debate it with her father in front of Hannah. Now there was no escaping from Trace's anger bristling at her and Hannah's plea for her to come with them.

Maybe if she did go, and saw the camp, she'd be less against the idea. But if she didn't like the camp, then what would she do? Before yesterday, she didn't know these people.

"Please say yes," Hannah begged.

"I would love to go with you." Asia spoke directly to Hannah before looking over the girl's head.

"You know she's only using you?" Trace shook his head and continued muttering.

Asia shrugged.

"I'm not going without her." Hannah held on to Asia's hand.

"I don't have time for this. Both of you get in the car."

Asia led Hannah around Trace. She hoped he read her silent plea not to have an argument. They all needed to cooperate and get through this without too much emotion overwhelming the situation.

Asia sat in the passenger seat, mainly because she didn't have a choice. Hannah picked the backseat away from the driver's side. They both jumped when the driver's door was wrenched open. Trace got in behind the wheel. He barely turned his head to the side.

Asia slid her seat belt over her body and clicked it in place. She remained tense until she heard Hannah click hers.

"Thank you for inviting me, Hannah." Asia looked up at Trace and offered a weak smile. "Let's go."

He nodded, his lips parted, but no sound emerged.

They drove an hour north to the camp. Little traffic passed them as they wound their way up the mountain. The car's engine sounded loud as the paved road gave way to a rocky dirt road. The ride grew rough. Asia held on to the door handle for security.

"Are we almost there?" Hannah asked.

"Looks like you won't have to wait a second longer." Trace pulled into the driveway where a large wood sign announced the camp. He stopped at the massive gates secured against the uninvited.

"Looks like I'll be locked in."

Asia immediately hated the fortlike facade to the place. This didn't feel like any camp she'd gone to for the summer. She noticed the stern guard did have a gun holstered at his side.

"You are not locked in. For the umpteenth time, this is two weeks of boot camp. Get you in physical shape, teach you discipline and learn to be a productive citizen."

"All that in two weeks," Hannah said.

"Yes," he said firmly. "It usually depends on the person's desire to change."

"And when I come back, I'll be brand-new. Then you can show me off to your friends. I can stop embarrassing you at my school."

"Stop being melodramatic." Trace got out of the car and

strode to a man and woman who were waiting ahead of them.

Asia watched him greet the couple. They chatted for a brief moment and then Trace pointed to the car. Although she sat in the front, she knew they only paid attention to Hannah.

"I don't want to go, Asia," Hannah said desperately. "I'll hate it here. If I didn't say all those bad things to him, he wouldn't have sent me away." Hannah began to cry.

"Oh, sweetie, I know this may seem frightening to you." Asia twisted in the seat to see Hannah's tear-streaked face. "You've got to trust your father. You've got to trust that he knows what is best for you."

"But you're wrong. He doesn't know, which is why he's leaving me in this place." Hannah pressed her nose to the window, her eyes wildly scanning the vista.

"Okay, I'm not going to let you get hysterical. I know you're a smart, warm, funny girl. You care about things. You care about what your father thinks about you. And that's all good. I know you've got a good head on your shoulders. You'll go in here and do everything that you're supposed to do."

"You're the only one who thinks I will," she said softly.

"Now stop that," Asia scolded gently. "Your father loves you. All of this is as rough on him as it is on you. Don't *choose* to be scared, okay. And we'll visit you."

"I don't think they'll let you."

"We'll see about that." Asia didn't care what the rules may have stated. She'd insist that Trace visit. She'd suggest that she'd accompany him, too.

Hannah wiped her face. Her mouth quivered as she inhaled deeply, then exhaled in a noisy sigh.

"That's my girl. Go on now." Asia waited for Hannah to be the first to exit the car. She willed Trace from putting his dark temperament into action. Hannah needed to do this without any public embarrassment.

"Thanks for saying that I'm your girl." Hannah offered a smile, then her face grew serious. In her most dignified manner, she walked toward the same man and woman. Asia smiled when Hannah offered her hand first in greeting. The stunned expression on Trace's face was priceless.

Asia remained in the car, shaking her head in the negative when he motioned for her to come. This was their special time. She'd already muddied things with Hannah's declaration for her to be there. In these few minutes of farewell, she wanted it to be strictly between father and daughter.

From her vantage point, she had the opportunity to spy on Trace. His hand lingered on Hannah's shoulder, occasionally playing with her hair. Then they disappeared into the building. For a moment, she wished that she'd gone to see for herself what type of place it was.

She looked again at the camp's facade. She couldn't really complain. Efforts had been made to make the landscape inviting, with tables and benches surrounded by wildflowers that dotted the deep green foliage. Other cars pulled up next to theirs. Kids ranging in the teen years hopped out, pulling luggage. Some were slow like Hannah and needed encouragement from family. Asia greeted curious parents with a short nod and small smile. She didn't really want to engage in conversation. No need to learn what deviant things their children had done. Chances were that she'd find that Hannah didn't deserve to be in their company.

The driver's door opened. Trace slid in, slamming the door shut. His hands clenched around the steering wheel. His eyes stared straight ahead. The grinding motion of his teeth shifted the shape of his jawline. His breathing was heavy, with a slight hiss through his lips.

"You did the right thing."

"Really?" He looked at her, the pain vibrant in his eyes. "Now I know you're lying."

"I know. But what did you expect me to say?" She wrinkled her nose at him.

"I told her that I'd only do it for a week, then if it was really unbearable, I'd get her."

"That's a good compromise."

He put the car in Reverse and maneuvered off the property.

"My nerves are shot," he declared.

"Hey, I know a good spot where you could relax. And you can tell me about Hannah. Despite all the problems you've mentioned, I know there is that little girl who thought you were her hero."

"I'm looking forward to meeting her again one day."

Trace walked into the house that he now shared with Asia. He was partly preoccupied with Hannah and the camp, but as he stood in the living room with Asia, he had no choice but to be aware that they were alone. Plus she was too gorgeous and caring for his own good.

He took on Hannah. He could take on a devilishly sexy woman.

"Let me show you something," Asia said.

Trace wasn't in the mood for conversation. He wanted to escape to his room and let his mind rest. Instead Asia now actually poked him in the ribs.

"I don't feel like seeing anything right now."

"Take a walk with me."

"No." Trace's patience withered and snapped. He wasn't in the mood for any back-to-nature experience.

"I'll make you a deal."

"What?" Trace didn't like the secretive smile on Asia's face.

"If you take that walk, I'll leave you alone for the rest of the day."

"How about the rest of the week," he taunted. Not that he wanted her to accept his challenge. She didn't have to know how much he enjoyed her company.

"You would love for me to say that you don't have to be bothered by me for a week. I don't think that's healthy." Asia threw up her hands. "And I'll be bored silly if I don't have a partner in crime."

"Oh, so now I'm a buddy." Trace had never been picked by his friends as the buddy to hang with. He was usually the person for chess or, in one case, being the lifeline for a friend who was on a TV game show.

"Come on, don't make me beg."

"I'd hate to see that," he said with a smirk. "I want to stop you from nagging me. I'm here, ready to go."

"Good. You're not as stubborn as you pretend."

Trace now had the time to take in and enjoy the surroundings. Being forced to do so really opened his eyes to Colorado's natural beauty. Mountains in the distance rose out of the ground, emphasizing their prominence against the lush landscape. Vivid shades of green carpeted the area, broken up by splashes of purple, white and yellow flowers. Coupled with the fresh, clean air, the kick of energy felt like a cool, crisp apple after a hard workout.

"Considering my trip to Colorado was a necessity, what motivated *you* to seek solitude in the mountains?" Trace plucked a small wildflower and offered it to Asia.

She didn't answer immediately. Instead, she smelled the small white flower, twirling it between her thumb and finger.

"A recent layoff from a statistical health career, along with a little bit of this and that."

"A mystery in the making." Trace nodded.

"It's not really a mystery. I'm still working things out in my mind. Don't want to sound like a total flake who's coming to the mountaintop to find herself."

"A flake would be the last thing I would call you. I find you refreshingly honest and patient, especially with Hannah. Do you want to have children one day?"

"Yes, one day."

Trace hated feeling as if he had stepped into dangerous territory. He couldn't ignore the frown that creased Asia's forehead before she turned on a bright smile.

"I may want too much, you know, like a family, career, house with picket fence, nice car. Instead of focusing on all those things, I'm working on the career angle. Not by choice, either. I'm celebrating sweeping out the deadwood in my life. I have no plans to jump into any type of situation in the near future. Everything else will come when the time is right, I suppose."

"I admire that calm nature," Trace said, complimenting her. "True planner to the smallest detail," Trace added, pointing to himself. "I knew that I wanted to be a judge in high school. Then by college, I knew that I wanted to work at the juvenile level." He chuckled. "I hate to admit that I made a list of the type of woman I should look for and marry. Thank goodness Florence, my wife, didn't mind my many lists. I think I made her a convert."

Asia wanted to ask about his wife. The type of woman he selected as his soul mate would be a window to who he truly was. Instead she said, "Lists aren't a bad thing. Keeps life organized. I prefer not to have my life mapped out, but that means that I have to unlearn that behavior. Spent too many years willing to please."

"Sounds like we may become each other's motivator to go with the flow of the moment." Trace carefully laid out the invitation and tensed as he waited for her reaction.

"I like that."

Trace took the flower from Asia's hand and stuck it through her hair so that it added a touch of color near her eyes. Going with the flow was tempting, especially when he desperately fought against the idea to kiss Asia. As much as she agreed with his newly found philosophy, he wasn't going to risk crossing the line with her.

At the end, the walk helped Trace more than he was willing to admit. The air had a therapeutic quality that cleared more than his lungs. The deep breaths he took as he walked through the rugged terrain pumped energy to his stressed mind. With no roar of traffic and hordes of people, a peaceful vibe flowed through his veins.

"Hey, are you getting winded?"

"Not likely." Trace ignored Asia's hand. Climbing the hill kicked his butt, but he enjoyed the physical challenge.

"We'll only go to the two-mile mark. But there is an outcropping of rock that makes the view breathtaking."

"I hope there are nuts and berries when we get there. All this intensity is making my stomach rumble."

Asia dug in the fanny pack around her waist. She pulled out a small bag. "Here you go."

"Aren't you the survivalist?" He gratefully held on to the concoction of nuts, berries and granola. "Now let's get to that favorite spot before my lungs collapse."

"Getting used to this mountain altitude can take a while. You might feel fatigued, have headaches or dizziness, but I think our bodies will get used to it soon."

Trace wished he had practiced more on Level 10 incline on the treadmill.

Finally they made it to the signage for the lookout point. Another group of sightseers moved off the ledge, leaving Trace and Asia alone. He pulled his jacket close, but his bare head felt the brunt of the dip in temperature.

"You obviously know how to dress for the weather," Trace said, noting that the sweater she'd carried over her arm was now loosely cloaked around her shoulders.

"I learn quickly. Spring doesn't always feel as such in the higher elevations. Besides, once the sun is tucked below the horizon, the temperatures can get quite nippy." Asia rubbed Trace's arms vigorously. "I hope this minor inconvenience won't stop you from joining me on future walks?"

"Not at all," he answered without hesitation. Her smile had a way of inviting him to smile. Again, he marveled at her natural ability to affect his personal space with a positive, vibrant mood. He held on to her hands, as much for the heat as just wanting to touch some part of her. His grip, though, seemed to still her. He looked down in those dark eyes that stared back at him with open curiosity. When she sighed, his gaze shifted to her rose-colored lips. He leaned in and softly kissed her cheek. "Thank you."

"For what?" Asia looked at him with surprise. She cupped her cheek.

"Just thank you for being kind."

"You've already thanked me."

"Every day is a new reason to show my gratitude." Instantly he considered moving on to kissing those sexy lips.

"Guess I'll have something to look forward to." Asia turned her attention toward the landscape.

Their view spanned the valley where the ski resort nestled. The deeply grooved path of ski trails carved its niche into the mountain face. The trails seem to start in the clouds and plunge down to earth in dizzying lengths. Snow still capped the mountain peaks like a heavy dusting of confectioners' sugar.

Trace had no idea which direction Hannah's camp lay. From the vantage point, the trees covered most of the land. Various waterways peeked through as they snaked a path through the mountain range.

Asia scooted next to him, as they took a seat on a flat rock.

"This is an awesome sight." He was keenly aware that their legs touched. A heat, not necessarily from the close proximity, buzzed through him.

"This is my second time up here."

"You came by yourself?" Trace didn't know whether to admire this adventurous woman or get on her case for taking such a chance. "You're such a force."

"Hah! I've never been described as a force. Any such resemblance is all an illusion." Her face grew pensive. "Somehow I gave up my…being…my spirit, just handed it over in the pursuit of perfection."

Trace followed Asia's gaze outward over the valley. Maybe the pain of loss in his life stirred his understanding. He briefly rested his hand over hers resting on her knee.

"This mountain is where I leave my burdens. No man to tell me how to live. No family to sway my decisions. I can even argue with myself when I want to back down. My life has taken quite a few chaotic turns of late. Now I'm learning not to hold back."

"Must be in the planet alignment. My life hasn't been on a smooth plane for a while now."

"But it can't all be bad, right?"

"Right," Trace answered back with a grin.

"Would you believe I went to a palm reader? Wasn't intentional. But I saw the sign in front of a little cottage in town and before I realized it, I was sitting in her living room paying for the privilege. Figured there was no harm in covering all bases."

"And?"

"I'll never tell. But give me your palm," Asia ordered.

He hesitated. Sitting next to her was like getting electric shocks intermittently. Her scent had a seductive allure. In her company, he relaxed and looked forward to sharing thoughts and the occasional laugh. More than anything, he caught himself admiring her as a woman with full-bodied sensual power.

"Don't be a chicken."

He lightly rested his hand in hers.

Her fingers fluttered under his hand. He resisted the urge to withdraw. He didn't really want to remove it from the warmth of her hand. What he wanted to do was to intertwine his fingers with hers.

He closed his eyes a brief second to push away such desires. The last thing he needed was to make her feel uncomfortable with his presence. His attraction had to remain well below the surface.

"You've got a strong, wide palm. Fingers are sturdy, creative, long."

"Will I win the lottery?"

"Long lifeline. One child," she remarked.

"Oh, like that's special information."

"But you could have many more."

"Fat chance." Trace tried to pull his hand away. But Asia held on to his wrist.

"I see something else." She lowered her head within an inch from his palm.

Trace tried to see around her head. He felt her breath against his skin. The soft scent of her hair filled his nostrils. He tried once more to pull away his hand. Thankfully she couldn't see the torture she caused him.

"Don't you want to know what I see?" She glanced up at him. Her look of something exciting, maybe flirtatious, teased him.

He gulped.

"A man who doesn't know when his leg's being pulled."

Seconds passed before he got the fact that she was kidding with him. She'd been playing. All the attraction and electricity had been in his imagination, and quite one-sided. He felt a bit foolish because of his reaction.

"Let's head back. I'm expecting Hannah to send me a text sometime this afternoon. And I left the phone." Thinking about Hannah pushed away any regrets of what he thought had been happening between him and Asia. Besides, the harsh reality had a bite that sullied his mood.

Asia emerged from her long shower with no clearer an idea of why Trace's mood went south. A little game with the palm reading went over like a ton of bricks. Maybe her silly behavior turned him off; although she wasn't exactly trying to elicit a certain reaction. At the very least, she enjoyed and was contented with a casual touch.

Her phone rang. She glanced at the number displayed in the tiny window. She popped the cell phone open and pressed Talk quickly before the call disappeared into her voice mail system.

"Athena, is that you?"

"Hey, sis. Just checking on you."

"Good to hear your voice." Her twin always had the

penchant for calling or popping into her life at the right time.

"What's the matter?"

"Nothing. Turn down your bloodhound senses for one minute."

"I'm waiting."

"I just came back from a walk. Maybe that's why I sound strange. You know, the mountain air messed with our lungs."

"*Our* lungs?"

Asia gritted her teeth at the stupid slip. Now her sister fastened on with the tenacity of a mother hen, pecking at her until she blabbed. Normally, she didn't mind a good gossip. But she hadn't quite worked things out in her mind to hand it over to Athena for microscopic examination.

"I'm waiting. And make it good."

"I'm fine. Glad you took a moment out of your do-gooder lifestyle to check up on little ol' me."

"The school is hitting its stride. New grant money has come in for equipment and expansion for more classrooms. Collin is looking into opening a high school. Life is beyond hectic. Plus there's still the wedding to happen."

Asia relaxed as her twin recapped the successful year of the school. She didn't have to probe about the new relationship, either. Once Collin had asked her to marry him, her sister had incorporated all her sorority sisters' help in planning the perfect Caribbean wedding.

"Asia? Are you paying attention?"

"Yes. Yes, I'm here."

"Well, who's the guy?"

Asia told Athena about Trace, but edited out any information that made her sound as if she didn't have a handle on her feelings. Not that her elusive behavior would really matter.

Athena tended to know what she was thinking or wanted to say.

"You got pretty nervy on me. Can't believe you allowed a stranger and his daughter to stay with you? Haven't you seen those crime dramas and documentaries? What if they were scam artists?"

"He's a judge. Even the rental associate knew this."

"A-ha. Are they paying you?"

"No. I said it was okay. The place was already paid for. And he's in a bit of a spot since his daughter had to be enrolled in a camp."

"All the way from Georgia to Colorado? What's so special about this camp?"

Asia bit her lip. There was no way that she was going to let Trace be judged by Hannah's actions. Nor did she want Hannah to be judged by Trace's decision.

"I know in my bones that you aren't telling me everything, but I won't push. You call me when you're ready to spill, okay?"

Asia hung up. She was a bit surprised that Athena backed off. But she needed to clear her thoughts and put them in order. However, that meant she would have to rationalize. How could she? This was all on instinct. Feelings. Her gut.

She emerged from the bedroom and stood at the balustrade that overlooked the living area. No sign of Trace. She listened, but heard nothing.

The camp, the walk and the burdens that she was sure he carried must have worn him out. While he rested, she'd straighten up Hannah's room.

She pushed open the door and surveyed the room. Hannah had made up the bed. On the pillow was a handwritten note. She moved closer to read.

Asia, thank you for being a friend.

"Oh, honey, thank you." Asia's eyes welled. The note touched her in its simplicity. She wished that getting to know Hannah better could've been an option.

"There you are." Trace's voice behind her broke the silence.

Asia tried to blink away the tears, but a few escaped, marking a path down her cheeks. She brushed them away. "I didn't hear you come in."

"I thought that Hannah may have left the room in chaos, so I came up to fix anything that was out of place." He stepped next to her. Although she'd wiped her eyes, she saw him scan her face.

"No chaos. She left the room pretty clean."

"Good." He raised his hand to her face, paused, then let it drop. "She makes an impression, doesn't she?"

Asia nodded. "Seems strange to me, considering the short time. I'm sure it's strange for her, too. I don't think, at this point in her life, she's used to people approaching her to be friends."

"I agree. Thank you for that. A part of her will always be daddy's girl to me.

"And another part of me is in bewilderment. Maybe your open, sensitive nature can destroy the anger and futility that I muddle through on a daily basis."

Asia hooked her arm through Trace's. "You've got to be a hard-nosed judge. No mushiness allowed."

"Keep that a secret. What do you want to do?"

A loaded question that conjured thoughts that may need an adult rating. But Trace didn't look as if he meant anything flirtatious. And that was a shame.

"We can eat and then dance until the sun sets," Asia proposed.

"I can eat, but I don't know about dancing."

"You don't know how to dance? I thought all judges danced in their chambers," she teased.

"Funny. I can slow dance, but don't expect me to do any hip-hop or break-dancing stuff."

"Okay, now you sound old as dirt. You're mixing your dance eras. Don't worry, this is more like a country-western place."

"Country-western place? Woman, is there anything average about you? Does a pizza joint with piped-in music not do anything for you?"

"We're in this beautiful place. Why let it go to waste? There is so much to see and do here. And we have limited time."

"I agree. But that pizza place might be jamming."

"How about my country-western place tonight?"

"I like that." He looked at Asia. "I like the idea of dinner with you tomorrow."

Asia blushed, heat warmed her cheeks. She pulled at her collar. Maybe Trace did know how to flirt. Maybe he was kidding about not dancing. She was willing to find out.

She stepped away, mainly to get a deep breath of air without Trace to short-circuit her senses any further. Casually she placed her hand at the base of her neck. Not only did her breathing increase, but her pulse also ticked at a lively pace. Trace had the power to cause physical reactions.

If this phenomenon stopped here, she could blame it on the drought in her dating history. But the desire to be around him also stemmed from their lively conversations. They had a similar take on politics, athletes and their sports and reality shows. The way his face lit up when he talked about his parents revealed a man who worked to make them proud and want for nothing. All these qualities and more were tantalizing samples of who he may be. She wanted him in her life, but didn't quite know how to make it happen without coming across as common.

An hour later, they arrived at a restaurant.

"Maybe we should've made a reservation?" Trace didn't want to admit to his own reservation at going to dinner.

"They don't take reservations." Asia took his hand. "We'll get an available table."

Trace looked down at his hand, then at Asia's profile. She swung his hand as if they were casual friends out for a stroll. After everything she'd done for him in such a short time, he counted her as a friend. He submitted to her wish for him to relax.

They didn't have to wait more than five minutes, when the hostess seated them on the outdoor deck, where there were only a few tables. They could enjoy their unique seats without the loud chatter from other patrons.

Trace scanned the menu, occasionally looking at Asia over the top of the oversize placard. She looked as if nothing fazed her. Meanwhile he felt like a teen on his first date.

After Asia placed her order, he went for the buffalo burgers.

"Don't get shy on me," Asia coaxed him.

"I'm so used to being alone that I forget to speak sometimes. I know Hannah probably wishes that I wouldn't speak at all." He hated the sad note in his voice. Lately, anytime he spoke about Hannah, he couldn't help feeling like a disappointment.

"Let's make a deal. While we're in each other's company, let's fill the space with our wonderful voices."

"You want me to talk about myself." Trace pushed aside his plate and stretched his legs under the table. "I'm the eldest out of three brothers. My wife died two years ago from colon cancer. Hannah is an only child. I was focused on my career. My wife stayed at home and dealt with Hannah." Memories wafted in, adding nostalgic flavor to his musings.

"She sounds like a great wife and mother."

He took a deep breath. "Yes, she was in my life at the beginning of my career, seeing me through the political machinations of the job. Then, when she got pregnant with Hannah, she became even more beautiful. But after she died, I felt lost." He paused. He didn't know whether it was cool to talk about his late wife, but she'd wanted to know about his life. He considered all the people who shaped him as important ingredients to who he'd become. "But she's gone now. I got a chance to say goodbye."

Asia signaled to the waiter. "Wine, please. Wine for you, too?"

"Sure."

They settled into a comfortable silence; the waiter returned with the wine and glasses. He left and Asia poured.

"I want to make a toast." Asia took the wineglass and held it up.

"To friends."

"That's nice. But let's celebrate *one day at a time*."

"I like that." He tapped his glass with hers.

By the time they were finished eating, Trace knew that Asia wasn't going to let him off the hook about dancing. He had agonized a bit, especially with the sudden realization that it was country and western. As far as line dancing, he could barely do the electric slide.

"I'm ready." Asia stood, adjusted the waist of her jeans, then hooked her thumbs in the belt loop. She tapped her boots, grinning with anticipation.

"I was hoping you'd forget." Trace didn't budge. Other

couples had moved into the center of the room, where a good-size wood floor was cordoned off for the dance area. He'd already stolen a few glances to see what the competition looked like. He had confidence in some areas. And he knew how to fake confidence in other areas. Dancing a two-step left his knees a bit wobbly.

"Just hold on to me. I'll lead," she offered.

"As if you haven't been leading all along." Deferring to her didn't bother him. She clearly mastered the dance floor.

"It's my secret nature." Asia threw back her head and laughed. Her hair fell across her face as she twirled in and out of his arms.

"Mmm. Actually I'm waiting to see what will set your world askew."

"Keep waiting. That is a very big secret."

Trace accepted the challenge. He allowed her to lead him as they managed a fairly quick waltz around the room. The close proximity allowed him free access to enjoy the beauty of her face. Her skin glowed, her light brown complexion was smooth. Perfection had touched her mouth, and it teased him every time she talked or smiled. All the nuances of her face moved him in an entirely new, refreshing way.

"You're not bad. I think you might have been playing a game on me."

"Not at all. You're a good teacher." He absently smoothed her hair behind her ear. His finger lingered against her ear-lobe. He may have been mistaken, but he thought he felt her shiver. "I told you that you may need a jacket." He pulled her close.

"Guess you were right…about one thing."

They danced, drank, and danced some more. By the time the sun had begun its descent, many of the patrons had taken positions along the deck. The tables had been removed to provide added room.

"Let's sit here." Asia motioned toward steps that led up to the deck.

Trace loved sitting next to her in the semisecluded area—it was a nice way to spend the evening. As the golden orb of the sun descended to kiss the top of the mountains, he also felt inspired to be bold.

"Asia."

"Mmm." She shifted her gaze from the colorful splendor. "Something wrong?"

"No. Everything is all right." He gave her a gentle kiss, deliberately designed only to show his gratitude—it was harmless and friendly. His lips touched her mouth, and immediately his stomach clenched. Nothing could've prepared him for the addictive buzz that shot through his system—he ached for more contact. He mustered slithers of restraint and hung on for dear life.

Asia turned her body to his. "Please don't stop."

He stared into her eyes as her hand went around his back. He covered her mouth, succumbing to its inviting warmth. Up close he inhaled the soft signature perfume that bathed her skin. He took his time accepting the invitation of her mouth, which was partly open in welcome. He'd wanted to kiss those full, sexily curved lips so many times before, especially when she threw her head back to laugh. Their tongues touched in a sensual game of introduction.

She pressed against him, crushing her breasts against his chest. He pulled back for air. His chest heaved. His head spun. She had the same effect on him as the climb up the mountain. Before his body's reaction could cool, he scooped her in his arms and delivered a kiss that had no time for rules of proper behavior. He devoured her, enjoying the soft moan that surfaced.

She pushed him away and kissed his neck. When she couldn't get to the place she wanted, she pulled his head back and sucked on the spot near his earlobe. Her teeth grazed his skin with a tantalizing tease that aroused him to the point of no return.

"You can't be real," he moaned. He kissed her softly and then pushed back.

"Let's just say the feeling is mutual." Asia leaned back, her chest rising and falling as if she'd run a quick mile.

"And that's how a sun should set every day of the week," Trace declared. His heart raced as if he'd jogged his usual cardio workout. No energy drink had quite the punch to the system as holding Asia in his arms did. He pretended to be fixated on the sun to avoid seeing any disappointment or irritation caused by his actions. Now if only other parts of his body would calm down.

# Chapter 5

Trace entered the living area, glad to relax after their delicious dinner. Asia must have shown him every landmark she discovered on the Internet. Her plan to keep him from being preoccupied about Hannah worked most times.

"I can't believe how cold it is. The temperature must have dropped five degrees." Asia pressed her body into the corner of the couch and pulled the blanket around her.

"The forecast did say an unusual cold front would pass through." He walked to the window and peered out.

"I've turned up the heat, but with these high ceilings, nothing is happening. Maybe you should close those blinds."

"I'll not only close the blinds, but also build a fire. Then we can camp out in front of the warmth and watch movies." Trace went to each window to seal in the heat.

"You're on a roll with the good ideas. We must have munchies, though."

"I've got that covered. I went out earlier to the bakery. I bought brownies, little apple tarts and a couple slices of a double chocolate fudge cake." He didn't mention that he'd asked the salesclerk for advice on what treats to buy for a date night.

Asia pumped her fist. "I'll have to work out for the next week at ten-hour shifts. You're dangerous."

"You look fine." Trace shook his head, and a big grin lit his face.

"All men think women look fine."

"I'm not all men." He looked around the room with heavy exaggeration. "From my point of view, I'm the only man looking at the only woman. You're fine. You've got the Cleopatra look going on, lying there on the couch."

"If I'm Cleo, who are you? And don't say Mark Antony."

"But, my queen, I'm one of many of your humble servants."

"Yes, but you are the most favored." Asia clapped her hands like a queen. When Trace approached and dropped to his knee, her giggling almost dissolved the queenly pretense. She held out her hand.

He placed a kiss on the top of her hand. Then he turned it over and placed a kiss at the base of her wrist. Ever so lightly, his tongue also caressed her skin. A spasm of desire shot through her. She involuntarily recoiled from his grasp, shocked by the vivid sensual slam to her senses and body.

"Fire." She gasped, licking her lips. Her throat ached from the sudden parched feeling.

"You're on fire?" he mumbled as he kissed her forearm.

"Stop distracting me." She pulled her hand away, tucking it under the blanket. "You have to build the fire."

Trace groaned, but obeyed.

"You were going to build the fire."

"Yes, ma'am."

"And then the brownies."

"Yes, ma'am. And after that?"

He started on the task of putting the logs into the fireplace. She stretched and scooted down farther on the couch. The man was pure eye candy as he bent and worked on the fireplace. How could a judge be so darn sexy and handsome?

He turned to see Asia's smile.

"What are you smiling about?"

"Just thinking if you knew what you're doing."

"With the fire?" He winked. "Or with you?"

A blush rushed to the roots of her hair. They had been flirting with each other, turning up the heat, nudging the limits. The old Asia would ponder her brazen behavior. Instead, the new Asia just succumbed. Pure enjoyment rushed through her veins like a drug that shot straight to the brain and started an addiction.

"I'll tend to the fire…first." He struck a match and lit the small kindling stuck between the logs.

The flames wavered, with small wisps of smoke curling up the chimney. After a couple of minutes, the flames grew stronger until the intensity was just right.

Asia didn't have to wait for Trace's invitation. She grabbed the blanket and, for comfort, pulled the seat cushions to the floor. After she had finished readjusting, she sat down heavily and stared into the fire.

"Meets with your satisfaction?"

"It's wonderful."

"I'll be back with the necessary nutrients."

Asia reached over and grabbed the cushions from the neighboring couch and dropped them beside hers.

Before Trace returned, she hurried up to her room. She ran into the bedroom and examined her face in the mirror.

Not that she was going to wear makeup to sit in front of the fire. But still, she smoothed her eyebrows, sprayed a touch of lavender in the air and walked through. She'd already changed into her comfortable lounging pants and T-shirt, and her feet were encased in bedroom slippers. She headed for the door, but paused.

*Should she do it?*

She could hear Trace whistling in the kitchen, still preparing the decadent dessert feast.

*What if she was jumping the gun?*

Then she heard the cabinet doors open and the clink of glasses.

*But they were really digging each other.*

There was the pop of a cork.

Maybe she could slip it in her pocket as a proactive approach. She danced around between the hallway and her room, biting her lip, trying to muster the guts to go retrieve the gifts from her sorors. She quickly stashed two in her pockets.

"Asia, where'd you run off to?"

Taking a deep breath, Asia joined Trace in front of the fire.

"This is beautiful," she complimented.

Desserts were grouped together on small plates. Flower petals were strewn around the cushions, filling the air with the strong, vibrant smell of roses. Music played softly through the sound system.

"Romantic."

"Not yet." Trace walked over to the light switches and flicked off a couple. "Now that's better."

Asia reclined, propping her body on her elbow. The dimmed lights were nice, but the lit candles set off the romantic setting in a warm glow. Asia settled down, lying next to Trace. Her body pressed against his while her head lay on his arm.

"Can I ask you something?"

"Of course. Go ahead."

"Your wife." Trace hesitated, and Asia was afraid that she may have crossed the line. "Tell me about her."

"I don't think that I should be talking about her when I'm with you." He paused. "Why do you want to know about her?"

"I wondered if you were ready…for this." Asia stroked his chin, tracing the square angle of his jaw.

"You are the only woman I've been this close to since Florence's death. I said my goodbye before she passed. We had a few months after the diagnosis to say what had to be said and what needed to be said. Don't get me wrong, the last year without her sucked me dry. But I had to think about Hannah. I had to force myself to wake up the next morning, make her breakfast, get dressed for work, go out the door. I needed a purpose for me and my daughter until the pain of loss wasn't so sharp. Now two years later, I am breathing in new life."

"Is Hannah like her?"

"She looks like her, especially how she laughs. And she used to like reading, something her mother did all the time."

"Have you told her how much she is like her?"

"No." He sighed. "She hasn't really wanted to talk about her mother. She has mixed feelings about remembering her. On the one hand, she's afraid that she may get ill like her. On the other hand, she demands that I not forget her."

"So much for a child to handle," Asia said sympathetically.

"And yet, what I've seen come through my courtrooms

would make our problem a light matinee special." He closed his eyes at the memories.

Asia studied his profile—strong, sculpted, defined. She wanted to touch his forehead and trace the strong lines of his face to his chin. She wanted to touch his skin, craving the spark that she knew existed between them. Lying next to him generated new vibrant feelings that moved beyond the mind to someplace within.

"You're quiet," Trace said.

"Don't mean to be. Soaking in everything that you shared with me."

"Holy smokes. Now you're judging me?" He rolled onto his side so that Asia's head was pressed against his chest.

"Aren't you judging me?"

Trace didn't respond immediately. "I think we're both guilty."

"I agree. I want to hear what you think about me?"

"I'm not playing that game."

"Oh, come on," Asia cajoled. "I'll make it easy. Top three things."

"Your generosity, especially with a younger girl. Your calming spirit, when things are chaotic around you." He leaned in. "And you've got a sexy body. From those gorgeous sexy legs to the tip of this beautiful nose." His breath warmed her face.

Asia swallowed. "But that means from my eyes upward, there's no hope."

"That's because it's all attached to your nose."

"Okay, I'll accept that."

"My turn. Flatter me."

"Confidence practically oozes, but no dilution with arrogance. Intelligent and a great fire starter. Last, and no way the least, a six-pack of abs to die for." She rested her hand on his waist and slowly dragged it to the washboard stomach area. His muscles quivered in response as her fingers applied soft pressure along the rippled panels.

His breath drew in sharply and then he released between gritted teeth. His eyes stared deeply into hers, sending an intense message that needed no explanation.

Hunger. Need. Satisfaction.

She read the signs and her body, without a verbal cue, answered like an apt student. No time to organize thoughts or sift through rules of engagement. She wanted him.

Her honey-toned, green-eyed roommate with brown, natural copper highlights in his hair offered himself. And she took the gift, in what was shaping up as a special night.

Slowly she ran her hand over his soft kinky hair, cupping the back of his head, holding him in place until she stretched her body upward. Her mouth hovered, doubt entering at the last minute. However, the desire pumping through her veins, the potency of her feelings, heightened her sexual needs in a way that she'd never experienced or imagined. She closed her eyes and his lips drew her closer like a magnet, until they connected. Her mouth sealed against his, kissing him softly, gently, with only soft moans of pleasure escaping occasionally. She felt his arm wrapped around her body, sliding downward to the base of her spine. He pulled her into him and she arched to secure the tight seal between their bodies.

She pulled her mouth from his to gasp for air. She opened her eyes.

"What is it?" he whispered.

"I don't want you to stop. I want more than a kiss." She grabbed his mouth to devour him. She offered her tongue, exploring and tantalizing him.

"And I want a kiss and then some...." Trace played with her mouth before he provided a deep kiss that created an explosion to the nerve endings deep inside her that ached for his touch.

His hand gripped her thigh and pulled her leg up and around him. He worked her mouth with his tongue. But he didn't mind multitasking, as his hand pulled on the drawstring of the lounge pants. Every time his thumb brushed her skin, she contracted and writhed, sending his senses into overdrive.

Trace wanted to be the gentleman, and was afraid of making a bad impression. Doubts filled his mind, but he couldn't stop himself. He'd opened up his life to her and her first step over the threshold impeded a clean retreat.

He tore his mouth from hers, sucking in air out of necessity. He admired her face, as he often did, because she had a beauty that originated from her flawless skin, which was the color of chocolate whipped with milk to a creamy perfection. Full lips sculpted into a pout and begged for his attention.

Greedy with desire, he wanted more than her mouth. He wanted to cup her breasts and lavish attention on them with his tongue, his hands, his lips. The anticipation of tasting her fired sexual messages to his groin that only barely held in check as his jaw clenched. Her hips grinding against his pelvis edged him closer to the precipice, until he grabbed her waist to still her.

"What's the matter?"

"I want you." He eased his body away from her, his jaw clenched as if in pain. "I want you so badly."

"Talk to me," Asia whispered, almost in a moan.

"But…you may not be ready." Or maybe he wasn't ready. A one-night stand didn't appeal to him. A holiday affair wasn't ideal, either.

"Thank you for being considerate." Asia leaned her forehead against the edge of his jaw.

Trace accepted the compliment. His dating skills had just

about dried up. Were there rules he needed to follow? Or was spontaneous the buzz nowadays? Being with Asia was like a free fall over a cliff.

He gathered Asia into his arms.

They gazed silently into the fireplace. The flames cast shadows against the walls. Logs hissed and shifted in the grate. The dry heat wrapped their bodies like a blanket.

"You know, I was looking forward to a night of passion."

Asia's frank statement snapped Trace from his musings. His held his breath for a second. Did he hear correctly?

"I wanted you to seduce me. Or I would have done the seduction, if necessary." She pulled condom packets from her pockets and let them dribble out of her hand onto the floor. "But you played by the rules." She leaned up, and blew an exasperated breath. "I know you're a judge, but I thought you hung up your robes away from the bench." She reached for a brownie, paused to study it and then popped the entire thing in her mouth. She chewed with her mouth bulging, shaking her head. "This took me out of my zone. I don't do this." Her hands splayed over the area. "I don't do this with men…or women, in case you wondered." Another brownie got devoured.

Trace didn't have to lower his gaze from Asia's rising state of anxiety to be keenly aware of the condoms that would have been needed if he hadn't stopped their lovemaking.

"Oh, good grief, you're not going to say something cheesy." Asia clamped her face between her hands.

"You're looking too adorable for me to stop you. Every time you make that face, your lips pucker with the sexiest invitation."

"This is not funny."

"Asia, believe me when I say that I want you with a desire

that borders on the wild side. But I don't want that special time to be mistaken as a jump on opportunity."

"You must have been a favorite of your mother-in-law."

He nodded.

"And given my current behavior—" she coughed delicately "—I'm the kind of girl your mother would have warned you about."

He nodded. That earned him a pinch. "Ouch!"

"So now what?"

Trace stood. "I'm feeling torn."

"About what?"

"I had no expectations...of us. I thought that I could go with whatever happened between us." Trace shook his head. "I can't."

Asia remained silent. Her dark gaze fastened on him, taking in every detail.

"I'm coming out of an emotional fog. You're recovering from a damaging relationship. Commitment is the last thing that we need right now. But I want more than you're willing to give." He raised his hand at her protest. "And that's not to pressure you."

"Are you for real?"

"I want a girlfriend."

"Like in dating. Going home to meet mom. Spending time with your child."

"Yes."

"Oh, man, this is heavy."

A phone rang. They both looked around, trying to pinpoint the sound. "I think it's yours." Asia pointed to the small instrument ringing and vibrating.

Trace hurried over and answered. "Sweetheart, it's good to hear your voice."

Asia's guess that the caller was Hannah was confirmed

when Trace started asking about the camp. She motioned to him that she was heading upstairs to her room. The interruption was welcome. Their conversation had taken a decidedly sharp turn down a road that stretched along unfamiliar, dangerous terrain. Did she continue blindly throwing away her inhibitions that she had seemed unwilling to cast aside? Or did she return to the analytical side that had guaranteed success in life, so far?

Downstairs a man stood ready to share his life and family with her. In the normal world, the storybook hero would be gobbled up by all the single women looking for a good man, but she only felt a strong fear. Her fear expanded as each harrowing factor fermented into a gut-wrenching requirement for her to commit.

After splashing cold water on her face in a final attempt to get her brain to think and issue a decision, she stopped weighing her options. Her biggest crisis was loss of work. Bottom line, nothing else mattered. No one should be allowed entry as she rebuilt her career and focused on rising to the top. The women in her family had never backed down from a successful career. And neither should she.

She shoved in the earphones to her iPod and selected heavy metal. Now maybe her inner voice would be drowned out from making emotional pleas. Or maybe an hour-long hard-hitting jog that blasted her muscles and strained her lungs would be the perfect anesthesia for being rejected.

Trace ended the call with Hannah. Hearing her voice provided comfort. He looked at the small screensaver of her smiling at him. Since she barely showed any teeth other than in a grimace, he had to use one that was several years old. Then, he was her favorite daddy. She looked up to him, wanted to be around him, and sought his attention. He slipped the phone in his pocket. Now he focused on picking up the broken shards of their lives and putting them together any way he could.

The two condoms on the floor caught his attention. He leaned over to pick up the objects. He looked up at the stairs, half hoping that Asia would emerge so he could motion to them.

However, she didn't stick out her head. Maybe she took offense to his abrupt retreat from their emotionally heated moment. He'd apologize later. But he hadn't changed his mind. He wanted this woman to be in his life beyond a fireside good time in Colorado.

He picked up the condoms and put them in his pocket. Hopefully, there would be a next time.

# Chapter 6

Each morning, Asia practiced an hour of self talk before she opened her bedroom door to head downstairs to the kitchen. She continued to feel awkward with regard to their fizzled evening. She entered the kitchen and immediately saw Trace out on the deck, reading the newspaper. Despite her plan to shrug her feelings off, her feet froze and her mind urged her to flee.

He waved with a bright, happy-to-see-you smile before resuming reading the papers. His reaction unfroze her feet. She got busy making coffee.

"Hey, good morning." Asia stepped out on the deck with two steaming mugs of coffee.

"You are making me get used to this special treatment."

"Don't worry, it has an expiration date."

"That's depressing." Trace tapped the chair next to him. He waited for Asia to join him. "I look forward to beginning the day with our morning chats over coffee."

Asia nodded. She offered a small smile. She really couldn't go on being uncomfortable. Because she didn't know how to start the conversation, she kept the mug near her lips for frequent sips.

After Hannah's departure to the camp, Asia and Trace developed a daily routine of sorts. Sometimes they talked until midmorning before they headed for a long walk through the state park. Today with the overcast clouds and rumbling thunder, a walk would have to wait for another time.

Trace folded the newspaper and set it down between them. "I don't want it to end after we leave here."

"We don't have a choice." Asia kept the mug close to her face.

"We always have a choice. Just depends on what you want to risk or sacrifice."

"I don't like taking risks." Asia shrugged. "And I've sacrificed enough, thank you."

"Who did the damage? Maybe I can provide sentencing," he teased.

"That sounds inviting, but I'd rather not waste any more time dealing with my past." The painful ache had grown distant and she wanted to keep it that way.

"How about the future? Feel like investing some time and energy for a good thing?"

"And what would be that good thing?"

"Well, it's more like *who* would be that good thing." Trace leaned over and kissed her with a tantalizing gentleness. "I feel those walls sliding into place to maintain distance." He tilted her chin up and peered down into her eyes. "What can I say to reassure you?"

"I think we should enjoy what we have here. Afterward, you'll go back to your world with Hannah and continue to rebuild your family. And I think that's something you should do without me clouding any issues."

"And what will you do?"

"Me? I'll be job hunting."

"Tell me about your career. Maybe I can help. In these times, networking is important."

"And you have contacts in Chicago?"

He nodded. "But you ever thought of relocating?"

"No." Asia had to admit that the thought had crossed her mind, but she never let it grow beyond a germ of an idea. With all the independence that she strived to maintain, she hadn't left her family or friends for longer than vacation breaks. That's why a year ago Athena's plan to go to La Isla del Azur unsettled her with feelings of betrayal, and some envy. Her twin had the courage to leave the familiar behind and forge ahead on her own terms. "Where would you suggest I relocate to?"

"Georgia."

"I couldn't. I wouldn't."

"Even if I asked nicely?" Asia wondered if Trace had helped himself to the bar before she served the coffee.

"But I don't want you to go to such lengths."

Trace brushed his fingers against her cheek.

"How's Hannah?" Asia sought a distraction from the heavy question that dominated the air between them.

"She's managing. I was happy to just listen to her voice as she told me about all the things they do in the day. Sounds like she doesn't have time to be moody or lazy. She asked me to stop by today."

"Really. Why didn't you tell me? That's wonderful."

"She asked about you."

"When are you going to see her?"

"At lunch."

"Oh." Asia didn't want to push. She expected Trace to invite her, or rather she hoped that he would.

"We can go for lunch together when I get back."

"Fine." She was irritated by the snub and by the fact that he seemed clueless of its effects.

"Great. It's raining again. So much for going for a walk."

"Maybe we could read. I've got some books in my to-be-read pile." Asia stood and gathered the mugs.

"Asia?"

She stopped but didn't turn around.

"I didn't tell you about Hannah because I didn't want her to be confused."

"Her?" Asia looked over her shoulder. "Confused? With me?"

"I'm trying to provide stability."

She looked down at her feet. "Got it." She shifted the mugs in her hands. "Tell her I said hi."

"Okay."

She went into the kitchen and set the mugs in the sink. She had to admit to feeling hurt that he effectively blocked her from Hannah. Her inclination was to force the issue. But why fight with Trace about his daughter?

From her vantage point, she watched him still sitting on the deck. He was looking down at his clasped hands. His body was so still that she had to focus on his eyes blinking to determine if he was awake. The pain he bore was only visible in private moments when he thought she couldn't see him. She wanted to ease the burden, but he wouldn't let her, unless she played along with his fantasy of building a perfect family.

She wiped her wet hands on the dish towel. She couldn't expect him to trust her when she balked over the suggestion to move to Georgia. She went to her room and picked up the book she'd just started. Now if only the words would stop swimming under her eyes. If only she could focus on the story because a part of her had latched on to the possibility. If only she didn't quake at the idea of moving to Georgia. The doubt constantly stirring in her mind got straight to the point. What if he rejected her after moving to Georgia?

Trace knew he'd messed up. His feelings were twisted into knots with no sign of an easy solution. He'd wanted to include Asia when he visited Hannah. But he didn't.

Was he punishing her? That would make him a control freak, a label his secretary attached to him with much eye rolling and muttering under her breath.

He went in search of Asia, looking into each room. Had she retreated upstairs? Was he so unbearable?

"Asia?" He started up the stairs, unsure because he heard no sounds. "Where are you?"

"In here." Asia's voice drifted down the hallway.

He tried to follow the source, looking into the other rooms and the bathroom. Asia appeared out of the room that Hannah had used. "There you are. What are you up to?"

"I wanted Hannah to know that I'm thinking about her." Asia pulled out a journal with a floral pattern on its cover. She handed it to him. "I'd given this to her because I'm sure there is so much going on in her mind that she may need to work out."

"That's very thoughtful." When Asia tried to leave the room, he stepped into her path. She looked up at him, her face full of curiosity. "I want you to come with me to see Hannah. Would you?"

"Are you sure? I don't want you to feel compelled to take me along. Having said that, I would love to see her. In a short space of time, she has grown on me. I don't have a younger sibling, so it's nice to do a little girl talk and share my insights.

Besides, I managed to wrench a couple smiles from her and I want to make sure it wasn't a fluke."

"I'm glad she met you."

Asia rubbed his arm, mouthing, "Thank you." She walked past him, but not before he grabbed her elbow and spun her around to him.

"What—?"

"Shh." He lowered his mouth to hers without further explanation. His logic and rules dissolved without being heard. He gripped Asia's shoulders, almost lifting her off the floor.

Her lips, soft and moist, enhanced the kissing experience to something that had the power to play havoc with his mind. He had no desire to rush. But he covered her face with smaller kisses, also returning to her mouth with determination.

She responded with perfect timing, answering his call to action with her own. He held her close to his body, almost going mad with the feel of her breasts pressed against his chest. Whenever their lips broke apart, he could barely stand it.

"Trace…" Asia whispered his name. "You can't do this."

"Why not?"

"I can't handle having my engine revved only to find out that I'm grounded." She leaned her forehead against his lips. "I don't know how to play by your rules."

"That's why I was looking for you." Trace kissed her forehead. "I guess my dating habits are a bit old-fashioned. I didn't mean to make you uncomfortable. I certainly don't expect you to disrupt your life to consider living in Georgia."

She placed her fingers against his mouth. "I need to apologize for my behavior, too. I caught myself acting too much like a victim. You don't owe me anything, including an explanation."

"Yes, I do owe you an explanation. And I really want you to come with me to see Hannah."

"You're not kidding?"

"Hannah would kill me if I didn't bring you with me."

"Great, let's leave in an hour." Asia planted a quick kiss on his lips and headed down the hall to her room.

He had wanted to tell her why he had been pushy, but he couldn't get his thoughts together fast enough to pass on the information. Or was he being a wimp? Deep down, he hadn't compromised.

Maybe this retreat in the mountains, shut away from normal, regular routines of life, suspended reality. There was no denying that a touch of magic was present in the idyllic surroundings. Otherwise, he'd have to believe that he might be ready to open his heart.

Asia walked with Trace into the main building to register as a visitor. The first thing she noticed was there wasn't any cool air circulating. The closeness wasn't unbearable, but she didn't know how they managed in the summer. Colorado still posted some large numbers during the summer season.

"Welcome to our camp. Mr. and Mrs. Gunthrey?"

"Ah, no. I'm simply a friend of the family." Asia took a step behind Trace to emphasize the error.

"Close friend," Trace provided, pulling her up next to his side.

After the initial discussion on Hannah's improvement and behavior, they waited in a room that was expertly decorated for a calming ambience. His face pensive, Trace stood at the far corner of the room, facing the door.

Asia empathized with his unease. She, herself, was nervous. Her hands constantly picked at her blouse as she sat on a narrow chair and also watched the door for Hannah's entrance.

Finally the door opened, slowly. Asia rose but stayed where she was until she saw Hannah come in. The disheveled youth she'd met at the beginning of the week had disappeared. Hannah's hair was in a tight ponytail. Her face looked as if it had been scrubbed clean, no heavy eyeliner in sight. Her mismatched outfit now had been replaced by a sweatsuit that looked more like a uniform than a personal choice. But all that didn't matter when the familiar spark of a fierce spirit twinkled in her eyes.

Hannah quickly hugged Asia before she took tentative steps toward her father. But his obvious joy in having his daughter in his arms overcame any hesitancy that either one may have felt.

Asia stamped down the urge to cry.

"Can you stay for the day?" Hannah asked, her voice heavy with hope.

"I think so." Trace looked over at Asia.

"I would love to." She didn't need Trace's silent message for her to decide to stay.

"Good, then it's all settled." Hannah let out a whoop before running out the door. All decorum disappeared because of her success.

"I'm glad you were willing to stay."

"Trace, you just don't want to believe that I want to be in her life."

"I believe you. It takes some getting used to. I have to think beyond the short term." He shook his head vehemently. "I told myself that I wouldn't broach the subject with you again."

"It's okay. I was thinking in the long term."

Before Trace could react, Hannah reentered, chattering at a speed that left Asia clueless as to what the girl wanted.

"Slow down," Trace ordered.

"Since they didn't know that you would come on our trip, they hadn't made any arrangements. But because I have an adult—make that two—then I can have my own boat."

"Boat?" Asia looked up at Trace. She'd done a cruise ship several years ago. But anything smaller made her queasy.

"It's a canoe." Hannah's grin never diminished.

Trace hesitated. "Do we have an alternate mode of transportation? I'd be happy to drive you wherever."

"No, Dad. This is important for me to do. We all have daily challenges to complete. I want to do this."

"Sure. Sure." Trace looked at Asia. "Do you want to stay here?"

Asia nodded as her stomach hitched. The trip was important to Hannah and they needed to be involved to show her that they had confidence in the program and in her abilities. She'd just have to suck it up. Hopefully her stomach would calm down and not embarrass her.

The canoe was sickeningly narrow, the length abnormally long and awkward. The camp workers helped push them into the deeper waters, for which Asia wasn't sure whether to be grateful or if she should jump into their arms as they waded back to shore. She sat in the middle, gripping the seat under her. She'd said all the prayers she knew and then some that she'd created for each rocking sensation she endured.

"What challenge is this supposed to be?" Asia asked Hannah.

"It's being calm under pressure because I have to navigate the canoe and be the leader on the boat."

"Just don't hit an iceberg," Asia muttered.

"I'm proud of you." Trace worked the oar he had at the end of the canoe.

"Thanks, Dad."

"Did you still want to come home at the end of the week?"

"I'm having fun. But sometimes I do want to come home." Hannah shrugged, but then waved off her contemplation. "The first day when I ran away, I didn't know where I was going. I just wanted to be gone from the camp."

"You ran away!" Trace stayed motionless with the oar poised to dip into the water.

Hannah rolled her eyes. "I didn't get beyond the front yard. Instead of kicking me out, they sent me to the counselor." She shifted her attention to Asia. "She's awesome."

Thankfully, Trace resumed rowing. Asia knew he wasn't going to let this revelation simply disappear. Maybe Hannah suspected the same thing, which might explain why she chattered nonstop about the camp.

"Why did you want to run? Was it because of the place or a person?" Trace looked directly at his daughter.

"I didn't like the place. I didn't want to be here. I guess I was afraid." Hannah didn't meet her father's gaze, instead focusing on her hands.

"The only thing that stopped you was getting caught," Trace accused.

Hannah nodded. The reality of her father's statement sank in. "I was scared."

"I think that's a normal reaction." Asia couldn't help it, she wanted to contribute to this discussion. "Looks like your courage kicked in because you didn't try to run again."

"Yes," Hannah eagerly responded. "I knew Dad would be angry. He'd be disappointed."

"You're right on both accounts," Trace replied. He set down the oar in the boat. Then he carefully scooted closer to Hannah. "Thanks to you facing your fears and sticking to the plan, I'm proud of you. I love you, no matter what. Even when I show my anger, I love you. Don't forget that."

Asia's eyes misted. She counted herself lucky enough to witness a transformation within this young girl, and between her and her father. From the first time that she'd talked to Hannah until now, she recognized a unique level of determination. Trace's humility to share his feelings with his daughter increased her admiration ever further.

"I still have to meet with the counselor, Dad."

"When do I have to attend?"

"Probably next week. She doesn't push for the parents to attend for the first week."

"So I guess you'll be here for another week," Trace said.

Hannah nodded.

Asia couldn't tell if Trace had any issues with attending the counseling sessions. But he had to know that he'd have to go. She looked at him, but he had his face averted as his body shifted with the rhythm of the rowing.

Shortly they steered down the river, staying in the middle to avoid getting stuck. Asia turned at every sound, most of which were birds on the riverbank announcing their arrival. She looked down at the clear water, amazed at the size of the fish darting alongside the canoe.

"What's the prize when we finally hit land?" Asia asked. Now that she could claim to have risked life and limb for a canoe ride, she didn't need to extend the experience any longer than necessary.

"You're funny, Asia. We've fallen behind from the group. Looking at this map, we have a little ways to go before we stop for camp."

"Camp?" Asia moved to stand, but fell back down heavily.

"Careful. You can't walk around in the canoe." Trace turned his irritation toward her.

"Thanks for stating the obvious," she responded, feeling equally irritable at herself for agreeing to come on the trip. This was clearly a father-daughter deal. She didn't need to be there.

"Asia, I'm glad you came." Hannah smiled at her with a winning innocence.

"Hey, I wouldn't have missed hanging out with you." Lying with good intention didn't count.

Eventually they skirted the last landmark and came up on the group. Now they had to get their canoes to land. Asia saw people hopping out into the water and pulling the canoe onto the shore. She looked at her slacks, which were already wet at the hemline, and her sandals, which were not meant to be used to walk in a river. She didn't know that she'd be part of a crew sailing the Colorado River.

"Don't worry, you stay put." Trace climbed out of the boat and stood in the shallow water. "I got this," he told Hannah, who had one leg over the side of the canoe. Without breaking a sweat, he pulled the canoe onto shore.

Once Asia had her feet on firm land, her nausea disappeared and her thinking grew clearer. She couldn't imagine getting back into the boat for the return trip. Scanning the area didn't reveal any SUVs waiting for potential passengers. All the other canoes matched theirs in size. She couldn't jump ship.

"Why do you look so worried?" Trace had walked up behind her. "I was a lifeguard in college."

"And that was how long ago? They may have changed the first-aid information by now." She bit her lower lip as his body rubbed gently against her back.

"Well, when you pass out and I have to do CPR, we'll see how well I can bring you back."

She was tempted to fall out on the pebbly coast for an opportunity for his lips to cover hers. If he wasn't careful, she just might swoon.

"Asia, come with me. I want you to meet everyone." Hannah pulled at Asia's hand.

"Wow!"

"What?" Hannah looked up at Asia.

"I'm surprised, in a good way," Asia said, "that you're making friends."

"Okay, *friends* might be too strong of a word," Hannah corrected. A lightheartedness underscored her attitude, drawing a smile from Asia. "For the first time in a long time, people want to be around me. Can you believe that?"

"Yes, I can. I want to be around you."

"That's because you're an adult and have to say those sort of things."

"You know, you're too young to be so jaded. I'm around you because I enjoy your company, crabby as it is." Asia tugged at Hannah's ponytail.

"Well, they want to be friends because I've won nearly all the athletic challenges. I've even set a few records." Hannah offered her hand for a high five.

Asia complied with a loud cheer. Even Trace joined in the minicelebration. "Well, I'm all for meeting your fan base. Lead on, fair lady." She glanced over her shoulder to see what Trace was doing. He merely smiled and tapped his forehead in a salute.

Trace had to admit that he was pleased how Hannah took to Asia. The instant bond had seemed strange at first, but Asia's calm demeanor set his daughter at ease. Without any prompting from him, Hannah had reached out to Asia.

He observed how Asia maneuvered among the gathering,

shaking hands and sharing laughs. She threw her arm around Hannah before they both broke down into giggles. He slowed his approach, not wanting to interrupt their levity.

He wondered if Asia saw how much Hannah looked up to her. Did she feel any sort of connection? Yet, she resisted the long-term possibility of a future with Hannah and him.

Maybe he moved too fast. But he didn't like to hover over matters. He shoved his hands into his pockets and veered to where the staff was grouped. They were making a small campsite and digging out food.

"May I help?" He needed something to do rather than spy on Asia.

"Sure. Here are the containers with the lunch meat on dry ice. Open all the packages, then each child can help themselves," a counselor instructed.

"After they wash up," a stern woman interjected.

"Of course." The man looked at Trace and shook his head.

Trace only nodded. He had no desire to pick sides.

Once they had finished setting up the lunch spread, Trace had the honor of calling them to the area.

"Dad, I don't think you need to yell. We can hear you and I think the birds could hear you, too."

"Go make your sandwich and cut your father some slack. But first, make sure you wash up, young lady." Asia stepped close to him and rested her hand on his back.

Trace had to concentrate on not making his back twitch, not turning into her arms and not kissing her in front of all these people and Hannah. If Asia had her way, Hannah would never know how special Asia was in his life.

"While you are standing there admiring the trees, I made you a sandwich." Asia handed him a ham-and-cheese sandwich and a bag of chips. "They have lemonade, soda or water."

"Thanks for doing all this. I'll make myself comfortable, as much as you can on a rocky shore. Could you bring me a lemonade, please?"

She blew him a kiss with all the casualness of a "good friend."

Asia returned shortly with two drinks. He pushed up to assist her before she took a seat next to him. Hannah had removed herself from their company and joined the other kids. They sat in their own circle with the counselors, laughing and talking.

"Hannah is a remarkable girl."

Trace looked up at the woman who had spoken so sternly. "I'm really surprised that she's settled in so well."

"This place is like a time-out, of sorts. They get a chance to think and reflect without outside pressures and other responsibilities. They also learn to be more responsible and understand that there are consequences to their actions."

"Then she can leave this week?" Asia asked.

"I wouldn't recommend it," the male counselor said. "We have a structured program, so that every day builds toward her success. Next week the challenges will be more intense and she'll have to dig deep to understand and talk about her feelings. There will be anger and resistance. And she has to deal with the emotions that may arise unexpectedly. Since she won't be here beyond next week, I'd recommend that she continues counseling."

"But then there is the possibility that she adjusts just fine and doesn't need a therapist for life," Asia replied.

Trace detected a hard edge to her statement. Her arms were folded at her chest in sharp defiance. He looked at the counselor for his reaction. He had a nonjudgmental expression, as if he was used to parental resistance to his approach.

"I'm sorry. I didn't mean to toss in my two cents." Asia took a long sip of her drink.

"Please don't apologize. You made a valid point. Maybe when Hannah gets back home, she'll be more communicative with you. That's the crux of a lot of teens' problems. However, I can see that you have an open rapport with her."

"Um…Asia doesn't live with us. She's in Chicago."

"My apologies."

"Not a problem. I will take what you say under advisement." He challenged Asia to claim otherwise with a look.

Trace enjoyed the return trip to the camp. He was pleased with Hannah's progress. Meeting the teachers and other students reassured him, and also provided answers to many of his questions. He had taken a right turn on the path of his daughter's life.

Gradually he realized that Asia remained quiet—not sad, but thoughtful. She teased Hannah, and they conversed as he paddled.

"I'll head to the car." She shook her head when he started to question her. "You go talk to her. I've said my goodbye."

He didn't say anything, but hooked his arm into Hannah's. They walked to the building. He'd wanted to say so much to her. And now that the opportunity existed, he feared making a mess of the time they had together.

"I had a good time," he offered.

"Me, too. I'm glad you came—and I'm especially glad you brought Asia. She's cool."

"Yeah."

"We had a good chat."

His guard rose. "Really?" He waited.

"I asked her how much she liked you."

"Were you giving her the third degree? I'm surprised she didn't get mad at you."

"I was protecting you."

"Me? From what?"

"Women complain that finding the right man is hard. I think you're the right man that women would want. I don't want just any woman to be your friend."

"Asia is a good friend." Never mind that she practically broke his heart every time they started discussing the future.

"Uh-oh, that doesn't sound good."

"And you are getting in grown folks' business, young lady. Don't worry about Asia or me. Whether we continue to be friends beyond Colorado remains to be seen. I like our little unit. However, not everyone wants such a lifestyle."

"But Asia told me that she looks forward to seeing me in Atlanta."

"Probably when she visits."

"No, Dad, she plans to relocate and find a job in Atlanta."

"Really?"

"Sounds like you two need some lessons on communicating," Hannah teased and bumped him with her hip.

Trace said his goodbye and hugged Hannah. He could barely walk at a normal pace to get back to the car. He'd no indication that Asia had changed her mind. That was a big decision and he hoped it wasn't an impulsive comment to appease Hannah. If she was playing games with his daughter, she'd regret ever reconnecting with him and his daughter.

He wrenched open the driver's side door. He folded his body and got behind the steering wheel. He didn't know how to put out the question.

"Something wrong?"

"I don't know. You tell me." He turned to her, waiting for a confession.

"Tell you what?"

"That nonsense you told Hannah about relocating." Even as he said it, he hated that there was no basis for the statement.

"I'm not kidding. I plan to move."

"You are going to rip out your life from one place?"

"I'm not ripping up anything. I am doing this of my own free will and sound mind."

Trace chuckled. He started the car. The news still had to sink in.

Asia grabbed him by his shirt before he could shift out of Park. She pulled him down to her mouth. She kissed him, not waiting for his invitation. Nothing about the way she conquered his mouth, and teased his tongue with hers, reflected indecision. Her kiss was driven and precise, like a fine-tuned instrument that expertly drove him wild.

"Let's go home. I'll show you how serious I am."

# Chapter 7

The ride back to the house was interminable. Every traffic light worked against them. Asia had set the wheels in motion, and now she didn't want to slow down. If her actions wouldn't have caused a vehicular mishap, she would have climbed into Trace's lap and worked him until he was bone dry.

"Make a right here." She motioned to the narrow paved road that shot off through the woods.

Trace braked, but didn't immediately turn.

Asia looked behind to make sure Trace's erratic moves wouldn't have an SUV in their backseat. Thankfully, the road was empty, except for a few cars approaching from the opposite direction.

"What's down there?"

"Could you just turn the car before someone rear-ends us." When he still didn't budge, she grabbed the wheel and turned it sharply to the right. "Trust me."

Trace snorted.

"Fine." She reached between his legs and cupped him, noting the instant hardening. "I want this. I don't want to wait for another thirty minutes of driving. There's a spot that provides a nice cover, and underbrush for the bed."

"Outside? Where everyone can see?" Trace asked, his voice growing deeper and huskier, as if strained. Asia didn't let up on stroking him.

"We can also watch the planes land and take off. There's a small airstrip nearby."

"I'm sure there are security cameras all over the place."

"Maybe. Maybe not." She leaned over and blew in his ear. "Are you afraid of a little indecent exposure?"

Trace grunted. His hands gripped the wheel. "Maybe I need to call my mother and tell her that I'm with a bad girl."

"Why don't you wait until it's all over? Then you may want to rethink that bad-girl label." She felt the speed of the car increase and she settled back against the seat, trailing a finger along his hardened shaft. "Turn down here."

"How do you know of this place?"

"I took a plane ride on my first day. From above, this location is nestled between the mountain and the river. Fully covered and vividly green. It's like nature undisturbed."

"Well, I hope nature won't be too mad when we're rolling around." Trace stopped the car, partly off the road.

Asia stepped out onto the grassy carpet. She popped the trunk and pulled out a blanket.

"Were you planning this?" Trace asked, a frown wrinkling his forehead.

"I had this in mind, but you weren't cooperating."

"So now you're going to seduce me first with empty promises and now with your body."

"Look, I've wanted you since the first day you walked into my house. I'm not going to deny that. But when I say that I want to be in Atlanta, I mean it. I respect you for wanting to keep your family safe from the predatory female." She turned his chin in her direction. "We both have trust issues. And if you make me think about this any longer, then I'll be in the master suite and you'll be in the housekeeper's unit."

"Well…since you put it that way."

Asia got out of the car. The woods had captured the smell of rain that had washed it anew in the past days. Her feet sank into the soft earth. She left Trace in the car, not one hundred percent sure that he would follow. But she had done her best to warm him up to her touch. If he allowed her, she'd energize his entire body.

"You're not going to wait for me?"

Asia smiled before looking over her shoulder. She unbuttoned her shirt and hung it on a lowered branch.

"Need any help?"

Asia shook her head. Then she unsnapped her bra, placing it on the same branch. Without the cover of muted lights and flickering candlelight, she shyly kept her back to him. He touched her gently, sliding his hands over her shoulders. Asia closed her eyes to lean against the muscular tautness of his frame. Her head fit perfectly under his chin.

His hand crossed her chest to cup her breast. Her restraint melted in waves, from her nipple, which he playfully tweaked, down to her belly button, where his other hand rested with a continued downward path to the juncture of her thighs.

He kissed her neck. The rough surface of his grizzled jaw heightened the sensitivity of her neck as he planted kisses along her throat before sucking her earlobe. She moaned when she actually wanted to talk. Communication by usual means couldn't happen.

"I want to see all of you," Trace whispered.

Asia unbuttoned her pants and pulled down the zipper.

Having him watch her turned her on. She pulled down the slacks and stepped out before resting them on another available branch. The sun breaking through the trees warmed her skin as she stood in her black panties.

She allowed Trace to openly admire her. Her initial fear that he may not like what he saw was unfounded. His breathing quickened. Open desire held his body hostage. She hooked her finger in the panty waistband to pull down.

"No, allow me."

"Oh, the gentleman."

He knelt in front of her. She looked into his eyes and her heart screamed. Trace held her wrist and coaxed her down so that they were kneeling face-to-face.

His hands reached up and cupped her face. Then his fingers disappeared in her hair. She wrapped her arms around his waist before he took her mouth with a fierce attack.

She wanted him with equal pleasure. And she took his tongue, which plunged deep into the recess of her mouth, exploring, seducing, conquering. And when she needed air, he shifted attention to her neck, licking a path back to her mouth. His guttural moan excited her, making her moist and ready.

He lowered her down to the blanket. On her back, she watched him toss his shirt aside. She let her fingers rove along her body as a poor substitute of Trace's attention.

"My turn." He slid her thighs open and place his body between her legs. His stomach lay on her mound. She wanted to cry out. He rubbed his body against the moist sensitive folds and she arched up for more enjoyment.

His fingers introduced themselves to her vagina, tweaking her clit as he sucked on her nipple. His touch sparked life into the various parts of her body, and she quaked and shivered with greedy need.

Asia couldn't hold back and moaned her need to be satisfied.

She helped him shove his pants over his hips, barely breaking contact for the necessary adjustment.

As soon as his pants disappeared as an impediment, she wrapped her legs high around his hips. Her pelvis shot upward, seeking and crying out for attention. Her nails sunk into his butt, ready to do damage if he teased her any longer.

He kissed her shoulder, sucking and nipping the edge. Anywhere he laid his lips seared the experience to memory.

"Are you ready for the ride of your life?" He pushed up to put on the condom.

"Bring it on!"

Trace obeyed. He took his time entering, like a visitor to a new home. He waited for her to relax and open for a bigger greeting. She allowed her thighs to go limp, grinding her hips as she swallowed him. She wanted it deep. She wanted it hard.

His mouth covered her nipple. He sucked the nub, using his tongue to coax and tease. Her hands gripped his head to hold him still. She needed a few seconds to catch her breath. He refused to comply, instead moving to the other nipple, where he devoured her.

She arched up, begging him to push harder.

He lifted her leg, shifting his position to drive deeper. Their bodies hit a frenetic rhythm that built on each movement. Her insides awakened with an orgasmic burst beyond anything she had ever felt.

Her cries of passion tore through the woods. Some animal echoed a response. She could barely concentrate as Trace scooped her to sit on him. Using her thighs, she gripped him tightly, rocking to a beat that underscored the carnal desire they mutually shared.

Asia tried to gain control over her body. But this was no time for logic, as another orgasm shuddered through her.

"You're killing me." Trace groaned, his lips brushing against the soft skin of her breasts. "You're making it hard for me to…" His eyes closed tightly.

She could feel his legs tighten under her. He was ready and she wanted to take him to the peak and stay with him until they came down together. Asia bore down, holding his shoulders, and invited him to release.

Their combined explosion rocked both of them. Asia didn't move until her heartbeat returned to normal. Then she practically fell off to the side onto the grass, panting. She felt as if she'd run a marathon, but the grand prize was a heck of a lot better than a ribbon or trophy.

They lay on the blanket, allowing their world to settle back into place before they headed home.

"I don't think that you just came across this place." Trace lay on his back, while Asia rested her head on his arm.

"How'd you guess?"

"You are a planner. I can't imagine that you would blindly come here even if you did see it from a plane."

"Well, you got me. I did see it from the plane and then I came here to do some photography. And it matched an item on my list."

"This I have to hear. What list?"

"After I got laid off, I made a list of things I wanted to do before I…"

"Before you what?" He turned his body, trying to see her."

"Die. I'm sorry if it reminds you of your wife. I'm really—"

"Please, don't act extra careful around me because that will make me uncomfortable. I'm okay. Look, like I've said, I've mourned. She is in my heart, but I got to say my goodbye. Maybe that makes all the difference when dealing with death." He lifted her chin. "Tell me how getting laid off motivated you?"

"I'm used to my life being in order. Now I'm relearning what is critical, important, or nice to do if you have the time."

"And making love under the protection of Mother Nature made it to your list?"

"I imagined that it would be sexy, uninhibited, unique."

"Can't wait to see the other items on the list."

"You keep right on waiting." She rolled away from him before he could capture her in his embrace. One by one, she picked her clothes off the branches. "I don't know about you, but I'm famished."

"You did what?" Sara screamed over the phone. "Wait a minute."

Asia lay on her bed, just out of the shower and still glowing from an hour of the greatest lovemaking she'd ever experienced. Part of her felt the need to brag when she called Sara to share her latest accomplishment. She expected to hear the cheers, and if she was present, they'd be hugging and high-fiving.

"Asia, you there?"

"Naomi?" Asia realized that Sara had done a conference call.

"Oh, I'm here, too, sister, dear."

"Athena, aren't you teaching or something?"

"This was worth taking a break," her sister replied.

"And I'm here, too," Denise piped up.

"No way, Sara, you're crazy. This was so not worth

a conference call. What if it was supposed to be confidential?"

"Nothing is confidential in this group," Denise replied. "Everyone knew my stuff with gambling."

"All for your own good."

"Let's get back to Asia. I don't have much time," Athena insisted.

"It was unbelievably fantastic." Asia grinned. Her body retained the memory of his touch. She couldn't help but giggle.

"Are you insane? How could you do that?" Naomi asked.

"You told me to have fun. I had fun."

"But that's not what's happening here. You fell for this guy," Naomi accused.

"No, I didn't." Asia sat up, plumping the pillows behind her. She clenched the phone between her ear and shoulder. Her sorors, as usual, misinterpreted the obvious. "You told me to be wild and crazy."

"But you don't have a crazy bone in your body. Even if you tried, you couldn't be freaky." Her twin had to lay it out bluntly.

"So the only reason that you would attempt to be freaky is if you fell for this guy." Sara tutted on the phone.

"Don't you think it's too soon?" Athena asked.

"Maybe you forgot when I broke up with Jack, but I know it was a year ago."

"And you're not pining over him?" Denise asked.

"No." By the time she'd broken up with him, she had already dismissed him from her mind. "I don't need a man to make me feel better. We enjoy each other's company. We have breakfast, talk about what we're going to do that day, and about how his daughter is doing."

"Whoa. Stop everything. Breakfast? He's staying there?

Daughter? Are you playing stepmother?" Naomi's agitation had kicked in.

"I knew we should have gone with her. She's like a babe in the woods. This man had better not try to play any games. I will kick his butt if he hurts her," Sara declared.

"Any pictures of him?"

"Nope. And I'm not sending one."

"You're mean. Just use your cell phone to take a photo. All these tantalizing details of male sexiness with no photo to support the claims," Sara complained. "How are we going to meet him?"

"Let's have a conference call with him," Naomi ordered.

Asia giggled. "That will never happen." She sobered. "Besides, this may not last."

"If it's meant to happen, it will," Athena advised in her usual matter-of-fact way. "And if he lets you go without a fight, then he's fool."

Asia appreciated her twin's protective nature. "Maybe I'm the one who'll let him go."

"Does it hurt to even think about it?" Athena asked.

"Hurt?" Asia wasn't sure what she meant. Letting go would be the final action. Right now, thinking about their separation felt like a wound that wouldn't close.

"You don't have to deal with the aftereffects alone, soror," Naomi said. "We're always here."

"I know, ladies. You're the best."

"By the way, remember that job you'd interviewed for with the Henderson Company?" Naomi asked.

"Yeah."

"I saw them at the monthly sorority networking hour downtown. I mentioned your situation. She wanted to know why you didn't call her immediately. She's been promoted and is looking for someone to fill her shoes. She'll have to post the job and conduct internal interviews, but it's yours if you want it."

"That's awesome," Athena crowed. "I've got to run. Catch me up on everything later. Talk to you, sis. And please be careful."

"'Bye." Asia waited for the click as she disconnected. "Oh, I wish you hadn't done that."

"What? Get you a job?" Naomi didn't hide her astonishment.

"I might not want to do the same type of job."

"What exactly do you think you want to do? Because it would seem that you'd take the job you knew you had before you went off on some tangent," Sara lectured.

"Girl, are you sure you're okay?" Denise asked, concern lacing her question.

Asia ignored the question. She could remain quiet and not have to deal with their lectures. But she wasn't ashamed of her decision. "I'm planning to relocate to Georgia."

Naomi emitted a string of curses until she'd run the full gamut of popular ones.

"Are you done?" Asia didn't understand the dismay or alarm of her sorors. At this point, she didn't want to spend any more time convincing them.

Sara continued with her fussing. "I know you're going to hang up the phone. You tend to do that when someone is saying something you don't want to hear. But this is really important. I want you to think hard about the job. This is not the type of economy to play games and hope for the best. What is in Georgia?"

"Trace and Hannah."

"They are a family. You have yours…here. Don't turn into one of those women who runs behind a man."

"Sara, give me more credit. I'm not the type to lose my

senses. But I've been away two weeks. And in that time, I've thought about my life, what I want to do and who I want to do it with."

"Guess she is telling us to stay out of grown folk business," Denise remarked with a chuckle.

"So are you at least coming home before you head off?" Sara asked.

"Yes."

"Before you get defensive, I have one thing to ask of you," Naomi interjected.

"What is it?"

"Would you at least go on the interview when you get here? Then if you still want to go to Atlanta, I won't step in your way."

"Sure." Asia didn't want to hear about alternate choices that could take her away from Trace and Hannah. She had every intention to stay in their lives, but the odds were stacked against them if she tried to have a long-distance relationship. And what to tell Hannah? She'd promised and pinky-swore so many times that she wasn't kidding about relocating.

A knock on the door startled her. She held her hand over the mouth of the phone. "Come in."

"Hey, babe, I'm heading out to do some grocery shopping. How about steak on the grill?"

"Sure," she whispered, cringing inwardly that her sorors could hear him.

He blew a kiss as he exited the room.

"Hey, I'm back."

"Don't even bother to lie or dress up the truth. That man is living it up in that house." Denise hooted.

"Athena is going to flip."

"The same Athena who went off to a different country and

lived on the premises in a place we'd never heard of," Asia retorted. Was anyone going to support her?

"Just think about what I said about the job," Naomi said, resuming her nagging.

"You all really know how to kill a buzz," Asia complained.

"We love you, too," Naomi responded.

They all expressed their love before hanging up. Asia remained lying on the pillows, slightly stunned at the different path her life could take. The only solution that tweaked her interest required guts. She readily admitted that she may be lacking in that area.

She got dressed to prepare dinner with Trace. Should she bring up the possibility of a change in the plan for her to come to Georgia? And what should she tell Hannah?

Trace had grabbed the few items for the meal. He enjoyed cooking in the kitchen side by side with Asia. They could chat about current events, their lives, their families, and skirt any deep talk about their future.

As he pulled in to the driveway, he wished that this was the normal circumstance. Under the beautiful facade of a vacation, this had an unreal angle with a finite point.

He got out of the car. The front door opened; she stood in the doorway. Dressed in a simple white dress, she looked fresh and ethereal.

"Need help?"

"Nah, I got it." He pulled the two shopping bags from the passenger seat and headed for the house. "But I do like seeing you standing there—waiting for your man to come home."

She smiled, but didn't say anything.

"Ready to eat?"

"Yep. I've started the grill."

They busied themselves preparing the food. Tonight the conversation was muted. Occasionally he looked over at Asia and she seemed preoccupied. He'd even had to repeat himself several times because her mind wandered.

He tried a new tack. "Hannah will be home in two days."

"Wow. That means you'll be heading home soon."

"You, too." He didn't want to keep asking if she'd changed her mind. That sounded desperate.

"I think that I've bought about two suitcases full of souvenirs." Asia rose from the table and began to clear the dishes. "Many of them are for Hannah."

"I can take them with me. Not a problem. One less thing to move." He forced himself to stop talking.

Asia offered him a shrug. She didn't look at him and that caused warning bells to ring. He'd pushed and tested, but she didn't say anything to confirm his doubts. Maybe he needed to stop overthinking the situation.

He drained his glass and rose to take it to the sink. He watched as Asia opened the dishwasher and inserted the glass.

"What's the matter?"

She sighed. "Don't know. All this seems fleeting. I feel as if I've grown so much." She laughed. "I know that I'm sounding a bit ridiculous. Guess I'm getting emotional."

He cupped her face, looking into those dark brown eyes. She closed her eyes against his close scrutiny. Her mouth tilted up to his, an offering that he couldn't resist.

The soft whoosh of her breath rustled the sexual energy to life. He took a deep breath and landed his kiss like an expert pilot, smooth and full of impact. When she surrendered in his arms, he plied her with his tongue. His hands reached around her back.

He lifted her to the counter. As she perched there under the brightness of the fluorescent light, he unbuttoned her shirt. But she didn't sit still—she returned the favor by pulling his T-shirt above his head.

In no time they were undressed. Trace lifted her off the counter, holding her effortlessly around his hips. Where he'd left off kissing her, she'd taken the lead, peppering his face with kisses. A shudder went through her body. He held her closer, wishing she'd share the reason for the sadness she tried to hide.

They finally stopped with Asia's back against the pantry door. Trace retrieved the condom and performed the necessary particulars.

"I hate goodbyes," he said.

Asia shook her head. "Let's not say anything."

Trace kissed the tip of her nose. He made a motion of locking his lips and tossing away the key.

"One thing, though."

He nodded.

"I'm all yours." She pushed away from the pantry and pushed him hard in the chest.

Trace stumbled back. Alarm shot through his body.

She continued pushing his pliant body until the table hit him behind his legs. She cupped him with a tight squeeze.

"It's my turn."

"No. I'm in charge." She pushed him back on the table. She climbed over him, kneeling and waiting. Her hand continued to stroke him. He could barely focus as she played with him. He grabbed her wrist and pulled her hand away. She had him tongue-tied.

His toes curled in protest. She drove sanity out of his head. He had to fight to concentrate. But as she kissed him, making a path down the middle of his diaphragm, he wanted to wave a white flag of defeat.

She paid attention to every part of him with tiny moist kisses that instigated an explosive reaction within him. If he let her, she'd drain him to the point of being a blithering idiot. He cupped her behind and lowered her onto him.

He hissed as her warmth encircled him. She rode him, slowly, dragging out each movement against his pelvis. The beautiful arch of her body provided a central point for him to focus. His heightened emotions lifted him as if on a cloud, where he and Asia soared in their own world.

She leaned over him, her hair brushing his chest with the increased frenzy of their arousal. He tried to talk, but a hiss of ecstasy was all he managed through gritted teeth.

He felt her release before he joined her. His body emptied, draining with blissful contentment.

## Chapter 8

Trace didn't think dressing casual mattered. But Asia was right. The brand-new blue Dockers and white polo shirt provided a light shield of protection. After a sleepless night, he had to face the uncomfortable part of this program by attending one of Hannah's sessions. The good news was that they would go home the next day. He missed his daughter. Although she had her difficult ways, he was comforted by her presence.

"You know you're making me feel like a parent dropping off her child at kindergarten." Asia brought the vehicle to a stop.

"Am I that bad?"

"Kiss me right here." Asia pointed at her cheek.

Trace brushed his lips to her face. He quickly pulled back, not really wanting a public display of affection to taint Hannah's report. Right now he only wanted to think about

Hannah. Plus he was afraid of what his daughter thought of him in her therapy sessions.

"Call me when you're ready."

Trace stepped out of the car. His stomach immediately tensed. He clenched and unclenched his hands. "You can do this," he whispered, before heading into the building to the counseling services department.

As soon as he entered, the receptionist greeted him. Then she pushed a button on her phone and announced his arrival. He looked over at the chairs, but didn't really feel like sitting. No one was in the waiting area, and for that he was grateful.

"Mr. Gunthrey, thank you for being so prompt." The specialist emerged from an office. She was middle-aged and professionally dressed, but still looked contemporary and hip. She greeted him with a firm handshake and direct, piercing eye contact.

"Thank you." His gaze shifted past her to Hannah, who sat at the end of a couch. Her head was lowered and her hands were pressed between her knees.

"Don't worry, she's nervous, but fine. We were just chatting about how her two-week stay has been."

They entered the office. Trace didn't know what the protocol was, but he didn't wait to find out. He rushed over to Hannah. His fear was somewhat relieved when she jumped in his arms with a big hug.

"I thought you wouldn't come." Hannah squirmed, looking uncomfortable. "I didn't think you would want to meet with the counselor," she whispered.

"I promised, didn't I? And this is important for you. For us."

"Let's have a seat. We are going to chat about Hannah's thoughts on life after the camp."

Trace took a seat next to his daughter. Did he dare hope that she had been turned to the right path? The right environment made a difference.

"I want to try to go back to my school."

"I think that the report from here will help when we make the appeal."

"I'm sorry for everything."

"I'm ready to start anew."

"Like a vow." The counselor prompted. "Let's expand on that idea."

Trace settled back in the couch. He needed this help and he wasn't afraid to reach out. Hannah had such a brightness about her. She had ditched the dark, baggy clothing. Even her hair was styled loose, falling in waves around her face.

"What we've discussed is developing routines. Routines give a sense of stability, provide a level of security of certain expectations. Nothing elaborate. Examples include having dinner with the family, having homework time, participating in sports."

Trace nodded. Lately his workload had increased. "My mother-in-law helps with keeping the routine, too." His workload would have to change, but he didn't have any issues with shifting around priorities.

"What about family and friends? Hannah shared that you used to host a lot of parties."

"Yes, my wife liked to entertain. I didn't mind it. But she planned them."

"I liked them."

Trace had stopped soon after his wife's death. He needed to mourn and he was tired of the well-intentioned, but smothering attention of friends and family. He hadn't had a party in two years. Planning a party may be more than he was willing to promise.

"What about Asia? I'm sure she likes to have parties."

The counselor glanced at him. He saw her look at her notebook, probably trying to place Asia in the family lineup.

"She's a friend of mine."

"She's coming to live in Atlanta." Hannah looked at her father, her eagerness showing. "Maybe you could fall in love with her."

"We are dating," he explained. Although the counselor delved into their personal life, he didn't want to bring Asia under scrutiny with any reference that sounded like a fling. He didn't feel guilty about dating her, but he didn't know if others were ready to see him move on. And there was the recent unease that he felt from her. She wouldn't admit to anything being wrong, but there were too many times when she seemed preoccupied or dodged any discussion.

"I really like Asia. She's like a big sister. Or like a…"

Trace threw a worried glance at the counselor.

The counselor stepped up. "It sounds like it would be nice if Asia was in your life. But Asia also has her life and her dreams that may not include yours."

"She told me that she was relocating to Atlanta because of me. She didn't want to lose touch."

"I don't want you to get your hopes up, Hannah," Trace said.

"Did you do something? Did you chase her away?"

Trace didn't like the panic in her face. He didn't like the fact that she had taken her easy friendship with Asia to a level that may be a guaranteed heartbreak. "It's not like that, at all. We'll discuss later."

"Hannah, I think we are finished with your session. I want you to know it has been a pleasure working with you. I have confidence that you will work hard and make the right choices."

"Because I already have the tools inside me from my family and teachers," Hannah said in monotone as if she'd been force-fed the message.

The counselor didn't address Trace until Hannah had left the room. Then they sat silently. Trace didn't have a choice but to be quiet because the counselor was intently writing in her book. She paused and bit her lip as she stared into space, then started writing again. The pen scribbled furiously, filling up the page of the writing pad.

He stretched his neck to read, but the scrawl was a blue blur against the lined paper.

She looked up suddenly and offered him a small smile.

"Sorry," he apologized. "I got a bit nervous."

"Hannah is going through a rough patch with her mother's death, growing pains and general insecurity about the people and things that she is used to being in her life."

"You make it all sound simple, but it was a bit hellish for the past few months."

"And she needed to understand that she isn't the only person in pain. Or that she can act out her frustrations in a manner that will get her in trouble. I think the athletic challenges, assigned housekeeping duties and required workshops provided a structure that may cause her to rethink acting out."

"Anything else?"

"Be firm with her. I can see the need to hold her with kid gloves, but she's also testing you in good old-fashioned adolescent style. If you waffle or give in, then you will get played."

Trace chuckled. "I've always been accused of being a softie."

"One thing that I'm worried about is Asia. I don't want you

to think that I'm getting into your personal life. This is only about Hannah. I'm worried that she has so much invested in Asia being in her life. Dating is a natural process and phase as you move on with your life. But it also means that you may be dating several women. I'm worried that Hannah is seeking something from these women that they may be unable to provide."

"You're suggesting that I keep some distance between them and Hannah? But I want them to get to know her because ultimately if they don't like my daughter or respect her, then there is no relationship."

"Good for you. But I mean that you make sure it's a relationship that you have some confidence in before making it a big happy family." She snapped her book close. "I'm hardly the one to play matchmaker. I just wanted to make you aware of certain factors that could affect Hannah's emotions."

Trace nodded.

The session ended with Trace feeling as if his head would explode with all the thoughts tumbling into each other. The counselor didn't have to tell him that maybe he was moving too fast. The thought nagged at him constantly, making him doubt whether he should push for Asia to come to Atlanta. He texted Asia, letting her know that he was done. By the time he exited, the familiar car was pulling up as he stood at the curb.

"Hey, babe." Asia leaned over to kiss him as he got in the car. "How'd it go?"

"Fine. Her last day here is tomorrow." He looked out the window before leaning back against the headrest.

Earlier when they had arrived at the camp, Asia knew her subdued behavior worried Trace. Frankly she hadn't figured out a resolution for own dilemma, much less how to tell Trace. Now that Trace was back in the car, she didn't think that she was wrong. She felt as if an impenetrable wall had been erected between the driver's seat and his.

She drove to the house, hoping that he didn't have bad news about Hannah. Once in the house they disappeared into their own areas. Asia tried to be patient and not demand a reason. Maybe it was because she knew exactly what was happening. The fantasy beyond Colorado was all in her mind, as her sorority sisters had warned.

The next day, Trace left to pick up Hannah. He'd declined her offer to accompany him. When they returned, father and daughter were still excited to be in each other's company, so Asia deliberately stayed out of the way.

By the early evening, Asia wandered downstairs, mainly to see what Trace was doing. She'd taken a nap earlier. She didn't see him in the usual rooms, although he could have gone out.

"Let's go to the skating rink."

"Now?"

"It'll be fun, Asia. It's like the first time we all went out."

"Do I get dinner out of the deal?" Asia asked.

"Dinner and roller skating. Can't ask for anything better."

The last dinner in Denver with Hannah and Trace *was* fun. Trace went out of his way to be comedic, turning it on for Hannah's sake. He needn't have worried, though. Hannah hadn't stopped telling them every last detail about her days at camp.

Asia laid her hand next to Trace, wishing that he would cover it with his. But he didn't move to touch her hand. When she attempted to cover his, he moved it slightly away until there was a gap between the hands.

Hannah excused herself to head to the restroom. Asia seized the opportunity.

"I know this isn't quite the best time to bring up this matter, but why are you avoiding me?"

"How can you say that? We've been together for our entire trip."

"Whenever Hannah is around, you maintain your distance. You barely kiss me, much less touch any body part. I understand some hesitation, but it's escalating."

"I think you are being overly sensitive. And if I'm careful— not ashamed—then it's because I want to ease our lives onto Hannah."

"She's not a piece of Wedgwood china."

"Why are you angry?"

"I'm not angry."

Hannah returned to the table. "Are we about ready to go skating?"

A beat passed before Trace answered in the affirmative. Asia tried to get herself back on an even keel. Her emotions were fragile, but she didn't mean to sound angry. She didn't even know the source of her anger.

They headed over to the skating rink. If given the choice, Asia preferred to pack her suitcases for the trip home tomorrow. The vacation was winding down to an uncomfortable end.

This time, Asia watched Trace and Hannah skate. He had asked for her participation, but she figured he was just being polite so she declined. They moved together like the perfect father and daughter. Hannah performed intricate foot moves striking her independence. He played it safe, skirting around her with a hovering manner. And that unit appeared solid and impenetrable.

Asia texted her soror, Naomi.

Job still avail?

Yeah. Rdy 2 come home?

Yep.

Things done on that end?

Asia looked up at Trace and Hannah sharing a hug before skating to the canteen. Done, trying not to regret.

Then think of the good times. Hugs, soror. Life's good.

Asia wanted to cry. Naomi was such a sweetheart. Right now, feeling so confused, she needed someone to tell her that things would be okay. The Gunthrey family had been a fleeting, and memorable, time in her life.

It was almost midnight and Asia didn't feel sleepy. She had packed and repacked the clothes and souvenirs that she'd collected. Her flight at seven o'clock couldn't come fast enough. She'd sleep on the plane.

A knock on the door stopped her nervous tending to the suitcase. She opened, expecting to see Hannah.

"I brought you a cup of hot chocolate," Trace said. "For old time's sake, figured you could do with a cup."

"That's very thoughtful. Much appreciated." She took the mug, but not before Trace wrapped his fingers around hers.

The physical contact was torture, reminding her of what they'd shared. What she saw in his face surprised her. She touched his jaw, running her hand along his grizzled cheek.

"What's going on…between us?" Her voice caught in a choked sob. She leaned into his neck, craving the warmth of his body, loving his male scent. She raised her head and sought the sanctuary of his mouth. His lips closed to fit along hers.

She kissed him, falling in love with him all over again. Her eyes opened over the surprised realization. She pushed him away. Her breath hitched. She couldn't catch her voice to say something logical.

"I don't want to stop," Trace said, his voice sexy and low. He softly touched her mouth. "Can't stop," he acknowledged, shaking his head. He kissed her with such tenderness that the wall she had hastily erected as protection melted away. She wrapped her arms around him, hanging on because she didn't want to think beyond this moment. His mouth ravaged her, pushing forward with a sensual intensity that whirled her into a frenzy.

"I want you to come to Atlanta."

Asia didn't open her eyes. She wished that he hadn't stopped kissing her. Then they wouldn't have to deal with the reality. And now that she could admit to herself she was falling in love with him, she realized that she was moving too fast. What they shared here really couldn't exist outside this fantasy.

"Asia, look at me. We can't let it end here. I've placed some calls to help with the job search. One of the judges I know is renting out his condo. He's holding it for you. You don't have to worry about anything."

"You're making my head spin. I don't want you to take care of everything for me. I want to make the decisions about where I live and work. But mostly I want to feel that I'm welcome in your life."

"What do you mean? I'm here with you now." Confusion marked his brow with deep furrows.

"You have to take care of Hannah. You're on your way to getting your daughter back. I don't want to interfere with what you may need to deal with."

"I want to believe that I have my daughter back. I have to make changes in my life to be there for her, but those changes don't mean that anything has to change between us." He took her hands, clasping them between his. "Besides, you promised her that you would come. She really believes this."

"This isn't easy for me. I can't go blindly into looking for a job, finding an apartment and dealing with you."

"Dealing with me?"

"You know what I mean." Asia didn't hide her irritation. She had jumped impulsively into this position. Now she needed a break to breathe, but couldn't do so without putting things on hold, for a moment.

## Chapter 9

Back at home in Chicago didn't quite satisfy the part of her that craved a new beginning. Although she'd left Colorado two weeks ago, the moments with Trace and Hannah stood out in her mind. Those memories couldn't be replicated by any thing or person. She didn't know if she'd ever get over Trace.

Her sorors' idea of a fun night to pick up her spirits sounded like a good idea a week ago when she agreed. Now with only an hour to spare before they noisily marched into her life, she wanted to reschedule.

After participating in various heartbreak scenes with the others, she knew the drill. They would come over, start off with something neutral, and then wham, they'd turn the spotlight on her. She'd managed to escape their various traps to question her at length. Tonight would be the inquisition. No mercy to be shown until she confessed.

As she filled the various brightly colored bowls with snacks, the doorbell rang. She didn't bother to answer. Her sorors knew what to do. They rang once and then pushed open the door.

"Howdy, soror. What's happening?" Denise entered first.

They each treated her to their unique greeting, competing with each other by raising the level of their voices.

"Do you mind? The neighbors."

"Your neighbors need to move," Denise said. She walked over to the counter and lifted two bowls, setting them down on the center table in the living area.

"Besides, I think it's time that you settle down and look for a house."

"Great advice, Sara. She's unemployed." Denise filled her mouth with the candy.

Asia held up a time-out signal. "Look, before any of you say anything, I have an appointment on Friday morning."

"Oh, that's not good. That's like the day before the weekend. Folks interviewing are distracted. The last thing they really want to do is to hire someone." Sara turned to look at her, shaking her head.

"That's the dumbest thing I've heard," Denise said as she tried to pry the sticky candy from her teeth.

Asia listened to their debate without much interest. She took a bowl, hooked her arm around it and proceeded to plow through the baked nacho chips.

Naomi, who hadn't said anything beyond the greeting, leaned forward from her seat. "Cut Asia some slack. Let's look at the movie. What is the movie, by the way?"

*"Fatal Attraction,"* Sara supplied.

"Why are we looking at an old movie?" Denise complained.

"Because you all wouldn't settle on a movie. And instead of canceling, I took the movie from my collection." Sara grabbed the DVD and headed for the player.

"So is tonight's theme 'men are scum'? You know how you all get on your men-bashing." Asia rolled her eyes. She should have rescheduled this get-together.

Denise put her hand on her hip with lots of attitude. "What are you talking about? All of a sudden you can't participate because you're all in love?"

"I'm in love. And I'll participate," Sara announced, which earned her several groans from her sorors. She still crowed about marrying her college sweetheart.

"Don't even include me in any of your wild theories." Asia pulled her bowl of nachos away from Denise's reach. She started the movie and settled back on the couch.

Denise pointed the remote at the TV and hit the power button, shutting it off. "Well, that sucked like a whole lot. He cheated on her and she takes him back. Like what crap is that!"

"I loved it. He cared about his family. And this woman was going to ruin everything," Sara explained, as if they hadn't seen the movie several times. She looked over at Asia. "You're quiet."

"It's a movie, ladies," Asia responded. "In real life, his wife would have separated from him. He would have dumped the other woman and probably moved on to another woman. The child would've been shuttled back and forth between the parents."

"Okay, that's it. You're like the Grim Reaper." Sara crossed her arms. "When we talked to you in Colorado, you were like a giddy schoolgirl. The way you sounded, I thought you'd be following him to Georgia." She grabbed the almost empty bowl from Asia. "Since you've returned, you haven't talked about him. Heck, you barely told us about Colorado. Except for calling me Hannah a few times—I don't even know who Hannah is."

"His name is Trace and his daughter's name is Hannah."

"Oh, he comes as a ready-made package." Denise raised her hands in surrender at Asia's squint. "Hey, nothing wrong with that."

"How old is the child?"

"She's a preteen."

"Oh, my, so he's way older than you?" Denise kept chewing on more candy.

"No. And why do you keep asking me these stupid questions?"

"I'll back off, but I'm only concerned because as Sara said, you were so giddy and upbeat. Are you going to visit?"

Asia truly didn't know the answer to that question. She and Trace hadn't really dealt with any particulars after their lukewarm departure. "I think we both realized that it wasn't more than a fling, despite the best intentions. We are both adults to be able to handle it."

"A fling? That's not you, maybe Naomi, but not you. Don't let your pride get in the way of what you know you want." Sara came over and put her arm around her.

Naomi snorted.

"That's the problem, I don't know what I want."

Sara took Asia's hand. "Are you prepared for him to pick up a new relationship with a sexy, single and truly ambitious female?"

Heat suffused Asia's face. Even her pupils felt as if they constricted over the scenario. She had barely thought about how she would deal with being separated from him, much less thought about how he would eventually move on. For all she knew, he may already have had a woman back home and she served only as a distraction.

\* \* \*

Asia had had enough of interviews. She'd turned down the job offer that Naomi's friend had recommended. Nothing in the current job market attracted her. She could get by for another four months. She didn't want to use up her funds, but this time around, she wanted a job on her terms. In the interviews, she heard the unspoken references to long hours, frequent travel, high-pressure environments. Maybe the two-week retreat in Trace's arms had spoiled her for wanting to avoid the rigors of the fast-track career.

Since her other sorors were gainfully employed, she had no one to play with until after work hours. She looked around her apartment for something to do. Her place was obsessively neat. Just then her phone buzzed with a message:

Hi it's Hannah. Miss u. r u coming to ATL. Thought u wld call.

Asia had called, once. But she hung up when the voice mail played. She didn't know what to say to Hannah, after committing to moving. Plus she'd hoped that she'd have heard from Trace. His easy dismissal of her hurt.

Her phone buzzed again. Can I come to Chitown 2 visit?

Asia flipped her phone open to reply. Her fingers were poised a second, knowing that she was reopening her life and heart once she responded.

Hannah, good to hear from u. Maybe u can talk 2 ur dad about coming. Hope u r doing well. I do miss u. hugs.

2 late. I took the train to Chitown.

"What?" Asia couldn't believe what she read. She began to text, then opted for picking up the phone. She needed to know specifics because the minute she confirmed that Hannah was on a train to see her, she was calling Trace. He must be worried, if he even knew that his daughter was traveling miles away from home.

The phone rang and Asia willed Hannah to pick up. She would personally wring her little neck. Now she was a bundle of nerves over the sudden news.

"Hello?" Asia thought she heard someone answer. But there was a lot of background noise.

"Who is this?"

"Trace?"

"Asia, I thought that was you," Trace replied.

"I'm fine, but I'm afraid that I've got some unsettling news."

"Go ahead."

She nibbled on her lip, trying to find the right words to deliver the shocking news. But she didn't have time to figure out the best route to take.

"What is it, Asia?" Now his voice was laced with concern. But typically, Trace kept his cool.

"Actually, I'm confused now. I got a couple texts from Hannah. She's on her way to Chicago to see me. But you answered the phone."

"Hannah is sitting here. Hold on."

Asia could hear Trace asking Hannah where she was going. She pinched the bridge of her nose. Great, this was Hannah's brilliant idea to manipulate a thaw between them.

"Asia, sorry about that. Looks like Hannah was being silly."

"I don't think it was silly." Now that she knew that Hannah was safe, she didn't want Trace to end the call. "I'm glad that

I got to talk to you." Gosh, did her voice go up in a singsong tone?

"How's the job-hunting going?"

"I've been on interviews, even had offers, but…I don't know."

"I'm sure you will find something perfect."

Ouch. There was a hint of an accusation. Did she come off as a perfectionist? She'd rather think that she wanted things on her own terms. Anything concerning Trace did manage to make her think in convoluted circles.

"Thanks for calling, but I've got to take Hannah to a doctor's appointment."

"Is she okay?" Asia desperately tried to hang on.

"She sprained her ankle in gymnastics class. Just want to make sure it's nothing more serious. That's why we were home today."

"Ah, yes. I'm all turned around because everyone else is at work or school." Asia managed a small chuckle. She pressed the phone close to her ear to detect whether he also shared in the laugh. She couldn't tell.

"Bye, Asia."

Asia's eyes welled with tears. She barely managed saying goodbye, as her voice trembled with the pent-up emotion. Her vain attempt crumbled away, as she tried to pretend that she had not been affected by Trace and his daughter. What hurt even more was that Trace had moved on. She hadn't accepted the invitation to continue bonding with the unspoken plan to be a part of his family. As a result, a barrier existed.

Being shut out hurt like a razor-sharp paper edge against the skin. The wound stung and throbbed, reminding her that she caused the initial pain. How badly did she need to have things her way?

Asia didn't feel like sitting around her apartment. Having a pity party wasn't how she wanted to spend her afternoon. But crying on her sorors' shoulders wouldn't help because they would tell her to kick Trace to the curb and be the independent woman she was.

Trace kept his back to Hannah. She didn't have to say anything. He felt her anger. But he had his own anger to deal with after receiving Asia's call. He did what was necessary to keep from asking her to reconsider coming to Atlanta.

"Are you ready to go?" Trace pretended to look through the mail.

"Uh-huh."

Trace focused on the electricity bill, examining the envelope as if it was something he didn't usually see.

"I think you're mean."

And that was the declaration he'd expected ten minutes ago. But her quiet tone turned the aim more deadly right between the shoulder blades that made him twitch.

"Watch yourself, young lady."

"Why do you pretend that you don't think about her? You tell me to be true to my inner feelings. And I think that you're running from yours."

"When you're an adult and you've paid your dues, then pass on the wisdom."

"Why do both of you need to fight?"

Trace looked up at Marge. His mother-in-law had arrived. She'd popped in to see Hannah and spoil her with ice cream and vanilla wafers. He wasn't going to talk about Asia, and certainly not with Marge, as of yet.

"We're not fighting, Nana. Dad is being stubborn."

"Or maybe you're not getting your way." Marge bustled in between them and adjusted Hannah's blouse. "Why do you wear these annoying braids? You've got beautiful hair. You need to look like a young lady."

"I don't think anyone thinks that I'm not a girl."

"Watch your tone," Trace warned. But he'd much rather change the direction of this conversation. "Let's go. Marge, I'll see you for dinner tomorrow?" Every Friday, she spent dinner with him and Hannah when all their schedules allowed.

"Yes. I'll bring my apple cobbler."

"Yum. I wish Asia could taste your apple cobbler, Nana."

"Oh. Who is Asia, one of your schoolmates?"

Trace took two steps over to Hannah and gripped her shoulder. "Come on, Hannah." He pecked Marge's cheek and thanked her for coming over.

Trace did manage to herd them out of the house. He walked Marge to her car and opened the door.

"Asia is a friend that dad stayed with in Colorado," Hannah said, before waving to her grandmother and getting into Trace's car.

Trace had no choice but to look into Marge's face. And he didn't like what he saw.

"Oh, you have a girlfriend?" Marge's surprise also looked like hurt. She stood her ground, waiting for an explanation.

"No. It's a long story."

"Then maybe you'll tell me tomorrow." Marge's smile wavered before it drooped and disappeared.

Trace closed the door and watched Marge reverse out of the driveway. She didn't respond to his wave as she sped by. He sighed.

He entered the car, knowing that Hannah wasn't done with their earlier discussion. That fact didn't stop him from turning on the radio and pushing the button to increase the volume.

Hannah turned down the volume. "When I go in to the

doctor, I want you to call her." She handed him his cell phone.

"Why are you pushing this? Maybe she has moved on. Maybe I've moved on. Sometimes the planets just don't align the way we want them to, and we go on with our lives."

"At least try." She touched his arm. "For me."

"Oh, you little manipulator." Trace laughed. His daughter had him wrapped around her finger into a pretzel knot. Now he could only back away from the request looking like a coward.

They arrived at the doctor's office without any more demands being made of him. When the nurse came to get his daughter, Hannah turned back to him. She didn't move until he held up the cell phone, acknowledging his assignment.

He left the waiting room for privacy. Still he couldn't dial the number. He wanted this woman in his life. Hannah wanted her in her life. How could he mesh their wants with Asia's reluctance to be burdened? He only wanted to protect his family.

He pushed the phone in his pocket and turned to head back into the doctor's office. But he remembered Hannah's attitude despite her request; she didn't believe that he would call. She did everything but call him a coward. But she didn't understand the difficulties in stepping into a relationship.

He sighed and pulled the phone out of his pocket.

He returned the call to the number that was logged in his call history. He had to pace while the phone rang. He hoped that she'd pick up, but he remembered how their conversation ended and he really wouldn't blame her if she didn't.

The voice mail engaged and he left a message.

He snapped the phone closed and reentered. He'd done his part.

\* \* \*

Asia stared at the menu, but her mind wasn't on the Tex-Mex cuisine. She'd gathered her sorors for an emergency dinner. Naomi couldn't make it, but Denise and Sara were present. They tended to be the ones to play the tribal elders with counseling and support. Right now, she needed their matter-of-fact advice to quell all questions buzzing in her head.

"Please stop staring at that menu. I've already put in the order for you." Sara plucked the menu out of her hand.

"Now that you made me miss choir practice, you'd better start talking." Denise selected a couple of nachos from the basket and dipped them into the pesto sauce.

"I really wasn't planning to be out tonight. But something occurred out of the blue and smacked me in the face before I really knew what to do."

"Tell us." Sara leaned forward. "Are you okay? Please don't tell me bad news."

"No. It's nothing like that."

"Pregnant?" Denise popped in another chip.

"Good grief, let me just tell you." Asia told them the entire unexpected episode. "Can you believe that he just ended the call like that?"

"What did you expect? From what you've told us, he wanted you to move to Atlanta. So, why didn't you?"

"Hold up. You think I should go to Atlanta?" Asia turned to Sara for help. "What has Denise been drinking? Since when does Denise recommend running after a man? I wouldn't even tell you to run after a man."

"Running after just any man is stupid." Denise rolled her eyes.

"See!" Asia pointed to Sara for agreement.

"However, if you have strong feelings for him, that's a

different thing. Love can change a lot of things." Denise was being too blasé.

"Who said anything about love?" Asia countered.

"You didn't have to."

The meal arrived, which only brought a momentary interruption to the conversation. The taco-and-enchilada special would have been phenomenal if her mind hadn't taken flight. She needed logic. Her sorors had been body-snatched. She looked at Denise, and then at Sara, expecting them to burst out in laughter and say April Fool's, although the first day was long gone.

"You are in love, aren't you?" Sara asked.

Asia nodded. "But it's too fast. You're not supposed to fall in love like a high school crush. I'm a grown woman—"

"Who has never really been in love—Jack doesn't count. He was a schmuck. And if you'd asked us our opinion on him, we'd have told you to run," Sara said.

"But you haven't met Trace."

"Why do you think we haven't?" Denise hinted.

Asia's fork clattered onto the plate. "Please tell me you that you have not been in touch with that man?" Asia was past mortified. Her sorors had the tenacity to pull elaborate stunts, but this was a bit much.

Sara chuckled. "No, we haven't gotten in touch with him. But we have eyes and ears and the one thing you've forgotten is that we've had the experience of finding Mr. Right. We know what it feels like. We know the power of love and attraction. And we're wondering why you're so stubborn that you'd make yourself miserable instead of going after that man."

"Part of it is Hannah. I'm afraid that I may not be up for the responsibility. She's like a little sister to me. What do I know about raising a child? She may even resent me for trying to be her mother. Why put anyone through the ordeal?"

"You're jumping ahead of yourself. Take it one day at a time." Sara looked toward Denise.

Denise chimed in, "And isn't that what you did when you were in Colorado getting buck wild."

"No need to keep harping on that." Asia cringed. "I wouldn't call it buck wild."

"I won't embarrass you with the details of how I know you didn't play by the rules. But my point is that you may need to relax and let be."

"Wow! You all have certainly moved to the other side... and left me behind."

"So what are you going to do?" Denise nudged her arm. "By the way, she counted how many condoms you came back with from the trip."

"You're sick!" Asia shouted, breaking into laughter with them.

Asia contemplated her next move. She fantasized about going to Atlanta. Now Denise and Sara had given her the support she'd wanted. The validation set her world askew.

They continued eating while she picked over the food. Their conversation turned toward their own lives. Asia realized that her sorority sisters were living comfortable, settled lives with routines and plans that included their husbands, and not necessarily the group.

"I want to talk to Athena."

"She'll still tell you the same thing," Denise said.

Her sister had taken a sharp detour in her life when she went off to teach at a school in the Caribbean. But more than that, she had fallen for the school administrator, leaving behind her life in the U.S.

She dearly missed Athena. As twins, they had shared many experiences. At times Asia wanted her own identity, but at these crucial life moments, her sister's wisdom and perceptive skills were valuable.

They finished the meal and skipped dessert. Sara had to get back to her child. Denise had to pick up the dry cleaning. Asia thanked them and returned home.

She walked through the door of her apartment and looked around. Her mind conjured what the place would be like empty. Speaking with Denise and Sara had provided a release for what she really wanted to do.

Her phone rang. "Athena? Did Sara call you?"

"Yeah, what's up? She told me that you had good news."

Asia pressed her temples. Sara knew she would procrastinate. "I'm thinking about leaving Chicago."

"That's drastic. Is this because of the job situation? I'd hoped you could stay put, but if the opportunity takes you elsewhere, then go for it."

"It's not a job. It's a man." Asia blew out an uneasy breath. She didn't want to sound like a lovesick idiot chasing an illusion.

"And you're afraid, right? You were always the planner. Maybe this is the type of economy where you don't want to take risks, but you also don't have anything holding you back."

"My apartment. My car. My friends."

"You can sublease if you want that security cushion. You can take your car. And you know better than to think you are leaving us," she said sympathetically.

"Why is everyone telling me to leave my life to go after this guy? None of you know who he is or how'll he act when I'm on his turf."

"Probably because we've been in the same spot in life," Athena argued. "You may feel as if you are making a decision that is beyond the average human's comprehension."

"But he may expect too much of me."

"And I know that although you may be trying to decide where to take your life, you are also very intelligent. No one can make you do what you don't want to do."

"I really miss you. If you were here, I'd make you go with me."

Athena laughed. "Yes, you would. And I'd feel sorry for you and join you." Then her voice grew serious as she continued, "This time it's your decision. Your move. Is this man worth the sacrifice that you are willing to make?"

"My heart says yes, to all of the above. My head throws up my fears about commitment, instant family, stability. All the things that I thought I would have in my life by now. What if there are no real answers? How long should I wait to be one hundred percent sure?"

"I know exactly what you mean. I wish I was there with you. There's a fine balance between following your heart and also being mindful of logic. I would say think like our grandmother, but remember she eloped with Granddad. Could you imagine that scandal?"

The sisters laughed over the fond memory of their grandmother's retelling of her romantic rebellion. Asia finished up the conversation with Athena by listening to her discuss her wedding plans before ending the call.

After she took her shower and was settled in bed with a cup of tea, she finally listened to her messages. Shock obliterated any sleepiness as Trace calmly requested that she call him to talk. Maybe what he wanted to talk about would squelch any need to move. But there was only one way to find out.

She took a deep breath that barely adjusted her nerves. Not much could quell the sudden activity running along her nervous system. She pressed the button to call Trace. She'd withhold her decision until she heard what he had to say.

Trace answered the phone before the second ring. "Asia?"

"Yes." She sounded breathless and tried to swallow the panic that had her heart racing.

"Let me get to the point. I want to apologize again for Hannah's behavior. I know you must be very busy."

"I had just come home from some interviews. She didn't interrupt anything."

"Do you have a job?"

"Had a few offers. I'm still keeping my options open."

"Why don't you come here?" He growled through the phone. "I was trying not to apply any pressure. Please allow me to take it back."

"I would," she said in a rush. "I would be happy to come to Atlanta for a brief time." She didn't know how long her feelings would last, she argued to herself. Or if the intensity of her feelings would be reciprocated. Moving to Atlanta would be like dipping a toe into the ocean before diving in.

"Hannah will be ecstatic to hear that you're coming."

"That's great." She paused. "How do you feel?"

"I have always wanted you here, Asia."

Asia closed her eyes at Trace's gentle reminder. "I want to be honest. I can't guarantee that I can fulfill the tall order you want of me."

"I've only asked that you come here."

"You expect much more, Trace. Not that wanting a wife and mother to Hannah is wrong. It's more than that. Your goals were set a long time ago when you started building and growing your family. What if we aren't at the same place?"

"That analytical brain of yours is dissecting every angle. I don't have all the answers."

Asia heard the disappointment in his voice. Throwing

out her many roadblocks effectively dampened the mood.
"Trace…?"

"Yes."

"I might run if the pressure proves to be too much."

"I get it, your flight-or-fight response has tipped one way
more than the other. I respect you for telling me exactly what's
on your mind."

"Stop being nice." The more that Trace spoke, the more
she felt like a heel by putting up boundaries. This wasn't the
way to start or build on a relationship.

"You do that to me." Trace cleared his throat. "Whatever
you want to do, know that I love you. Bye, sweetheart."

"Bye," Asia whispered.


Two weeks rolled by in Asia's life with little progress in
her decision. She had everyone's support. She'd uttered the
words that she'd go, but no further action occurred.

Sitting at her dining table, she had two letters from
prospective employers. One letter eloquently complimented
her on her solid background in the health analyst field and
what contributions she would make to the company, along
with a confirmation of her large salary. The increase of twenty
thousand shocked her, but she'd played it cool when she told
them that she'd think it over. Now the company had also
included a seven-thousand-dollar signing bonus.

If she accepted this senior level position, her career would
be back on target. The career ladder would be firmly in place
and she'd have a good chance to soar. This kind of opportunity
didn't come often, nor was it simply luck. Getting her master's,
having a solid career history and earning a reputation in the
industry made her a valuable asset.

All she had to do was to pick up the phone tomorrow
morning and accept the offer.

And turn her back on Atlanta.

But she also had another letter that acknowledged her telephone interview without any major compliments. The short business letter stated that she had met the criteria necessary to be considered for a second in-person interview. The salary matched what she'd made, but there was no mention of a signing bonus in sight. This job offer would be considered a lateral move.

Asia pushed one letter above the other, then switched their positions. This dilemma should be a no-brainer. But the one thing that sabotaged her thought process was that the second letter was a job in Atlanta.

She'd rejected using Trace to help find her a job. She'd rather do this on her own. If nothing came of this major reordering of her life, she didn't want to feel obligated to him. Now her pride landed her a tentative option that held no guarantee.

As she always did, Asia made a list of advantages and disadvantages. Less than halfway through the process, she balled the paper and tossed it aside. The right thing to do didn't quite mesh with the thing she wanted.

She wanted Trace. She needed him. She was going to have him.

## Chapter 10

Trace took his seat on the judge's bench. His files for the upcoming cases were off to the side, in easy reach. His customary pitcher of iced water and a glass were also well-positioned. He noted, as the people in the courtroom settled back in their seats, that besides the court clerk, prosecutor and attorney, only the mother was present.

The sentence hearing had the potential to be very emotional when his decision was handed down. He allowed for the stories that tried to prove extenuating circumstances. He listened to attorneys who shared success stories of rehabilitation. And in extreme cases, he had to block some of the heart-wrenching stories to be impartial. Those stories came from the accused and detailed the type of life they'd had to live to survive.

"Lawrence Getty, step forward."

The rebellious teen stepped forward. His face was tattooed with what looked like Celtic knots along one side. He had a couple of nose rings, and his shaved head presented a fearsome image. Trace wasn't intimidated. Five years on the bench had brought all manner of social misfits and outcasts before him.

Despite how the accused felt about him, he truly cared about each one of them. But caring didn't mean rolling over and granting the opportunity to avoid punishment.

"Mr. Getty, you've shown no remorse during your trial. I told your attorney that you should write a letter to me, to tell me about yourself. You refused to do so."

"It wasn't nothin' personal, Your Honor. But if I'm gonna be punished, what difference does it make if you know about me or not?"

"You've had run-ins with the law." Trace flipped through the large packet of papers pinned to the file. "I think in one case, I even heard your trial. Now it's within my authority to toss you into juvenile detention for several years, and to recommend you for the Winfrey Renewal Foundation. The letter would help me to see if you are engaged in your own rehabilitation. If there is a glimmer of optimism that someone with the right touch can harness."

Trace held the teen's stare, seeing past the anger and curiosity, to the teenager trying to be a man. This kid was tough. And he was used to being treated with the harshness that came with a certain life. But he wasn't in front of him today because of jaywalking.

"How is Randall doing?" Trace asked the prosecutor.

"He's at home now. His parents have a physical therapist coming to the house. They have decided to withdraw him from school and homeschool him."

Trace shook his head. He couldn't let his temper rise.

"He shouldn't have smiled at me."

Trace's pen stilled. He set aside the paper that granted entry to the camp.

"I'm not a fag. He smiled at me. That's like an attack."
Lawrence's fist closed and his mouth tightened. "I ain't taking
that from no man."

"I think you should listen to your attorney, for a change."
Trace waved off the attorney. "You put a boy in the hospital
because he smiled at you. His sexual orientation, which you
only guessed at, was enough for you to put your hands on
him." Trace made a few more notes to the file. "Well, Mr.
Getty, you are heading for the Hodgkins Boot Camp facility
for their six-month program. Upon successful completion, you
will then go to the Winfrey Renewal Foundation for another
six months. If you are dismissed from the foundation, you
will return to the boot camp facility to finish your sentence.
Good luck. I'd suggest you use your time wisely. A separate
restitution hearing will be scheduled."

Trace banged his gavel.

Now he needed a drink of that water. He waited for the
courtroom to clear and the next case to be presented. He
scanned the file to reacquaint himself.

An older woman entered the courtroom, already sniffling
and dabbing at her eyes. He labeled her the mother. Three
mature women sat beside her. The ones closest to her rubbed
her shoulders and whispered in her ear. They must be aunts or
members of the church's women's circle. One man sat in the
room, but nowhere close to the women, although he appeared
to earn their glares when they glanced at him. Maybe that was
the father, who was clearly not welcome.

"Please step forward, Bowzer Simpson." Trace beckoned
to the youth.

"I want to explain." The boy—and he looked more like a
boy than a sixteen-year-old—was the model of a geeky school
kid. His acne-spotted skin was pink. A strong wind might just
knock him over. He couldn't hold eye contact, as his gaze slid

to some object off to the side of Trace's head. The trauma of his experience certainly took hold of him as he seemed to be permanently shivering. Trace didn't have to guess whether he was remorseful, but he didn't want him to ever forget this experience.

"There is a time for your explanation and this is not it." Trace looked at the attorney to send the message to calm his client. The attorney laid a hand on his client's arm, which seemed to spike his nerves even more.

"I have reviewed your file, Mr. Simpson, and you're here for sentencing. The trial is over. You are guilty."

"But wait, I want to explain," Bowzer squeaked.

"Go ahead." Trace folded his arms and leaned back in his chair. He'd heard the story during trial and doubted anything new would come to his attention.

"Your Honor, my girlfriend told me to come over. She wanted to lose her virginity." Sweat broke out on Bowzer's brow. He wiped it with the back of his hand. "We had a plan. I'd visit her by climbing through the window into her bedroom. But her pops was standing there talking to her. I didn't see him and fell in. Then she said that she didn't know why I was there." His face turned deep red, making the acne stand out. "Then her father threw me against the wall and threatened to throw me through the window. That's when my girlfriend called the police. He told them that I was breaking and entering. But I wasn't," Bowzer whined.

"Okay, I've heard enough. Mr. Simpson, is your mother here?"

The boy pointed to the woman he'd suspected was the mother.

"How about your father?"

The boy shook his head.

"That's the girlfriend's father, Your Honor," the prosecutor offered when he saw Trace look questioningly at the man.

"You, sir. You, ma'am. Step forward." Trace waited until the small group was in place. "Mr. Benton, I realize the basis of your anger, father to father."

"Well, Your Honor, I had time to calm down. My daughter is making my life hell…oh, sorry, Your Honor." The man performed a little bow. "I came to ask that you show mercy."

"Mr. Simpson, I hope that you have learned from this experience. You're one of the lucky ones who doesn't have a rap sheet. The one time that you allowed your hormones to rule, you did something dumb. Life isn't your playground, where you can do whatever you want, and when you want. *Consequences* is my favorite word. Since you have so much time on your hands, I'd suggest you keep it busy with one hundred hours' community service."

Bowzer erupted in a gleeful whoop.

His small band of supporters uttered cries of happiness.

The assistant district attorney just shook her head at him, a small smile that only he could see.

Trace knew she'd have something to say about his soft approach, but he was used to her ribbing. He closed the file, glad that he could offer a second chance.

Some of the later cases were too messy and offenders had gone down a dark road, which required a more neutral or hard-edged resolution. Maybe he should have Hannah sit in on a few hearings as a preventative measure and for good discussion points between them. He wrote a quick note to the bailiff, then declared a one-hour recess.

"All rise!"

Trace left the courtroom and happily headed for his chamber. He loved serving as judge. Despite the circumstances of the defendants who came to his courtroom, they made him feel connected to the youth. It was why he'd tried all those approaches with Hannah that didn't always work.

Since her two weeks at the boot camp, she'd come back with a maturity level that impressed him. Occasionally the petulance would surface, but he didn't have to be treated to one of her brooding, dark, emotional displays.

His secretary signaled to him. "Judge, you have a visitor."

Trace looked around the small area, then back to Katrina.

"I allowed her into your office. Don't worry, she showed me ID, told me a wonderful story and then I showed her in."

"Well, what's her name?" He held his breath, hoping.

"It's a surprise. She told me a wonderful story about how she met you." With a huge grin, Katrina flicked him away with her fingers.

"Katrina, no one is allowed in my office." He didn't wait a second longer. His new secretary had violated a key security policy. He hurried into his office.

"You know a girl could lose a leg in here from all this clutter on the floor." Asia stepped out of a corner where the file cabinets were. "Hi, Trace."

She stood with her hands clasped demurely in front of her. Her skin radiated with a sheen that highlighted her smooth medium brown complexion. Dressed in a natural beige ensemble, everything about her was flawless. He studied her, trying to discern what was different.

She looked model perfect. Fresh, sexy, gorgeous with a slight gold-toned makeup. Her lips glistened as if she'd sprinkled gold dust over her mouth. All he wanted to do was kiss her.

Her hair gleamed in its severely tucked upswept do. The

height elongated her neck, adding to the elegance. She could give the first lady a run.

"Come here," he ordered, his voice husky with emotion.

She walked toward him slowly. When she was only inches away, she took a big step toward him and threw herself into his arms.

"I've missed you so much," he admitted before covering her mouth with his. He tried to wrap his arms around her, but his judge's gown got in the way. He pulled it open and tossed it aside. He craved the touch of her body against his. He couldn't help the soft moan when he pressed her body against his.

While his mouth sought the warm comfort of her mouth, his hips closed the gap with hers. Her body molded against his, raising the temperature of his body to a sensual heat that would soon need something to squelch the fire.

"I thought you'd changed your mind," Trace whispered against her ear. He kept his arms around her, not wanting to let go in case she disappeared.

"I had an interview," Asia explained.

"I could have put in a few calls. You wouldn't have to put yourself through this."

"I know." She kissed his mouth, nuzzling his cheek with her nose. "I wanted to come out here on my own."

"You're stubborn," he declared.

He pulled out the paper bag from his briefcase. "Want to share lunch? Hannah made it."

"Well, this is creative." Asia held up half of a sandwich.

"Yep, peanut butter, banana and strawberry jam. She said it's full of nutrients."

"I'm hungry, which is the only reason that I will try this."

"You'll get used to it," he responded, but wanted to retract the comment if Asia looked uncomfortable. Instead, she nibbled at the edges of the sandwich.

"Not bad. Tastes better than it looks. Looks like Hannah knows what she's talking about." Trace dabbed at her mouth, where a speck of peanut butter stayed put. "By the way, how is Hannah? Will I get to see her tonight or is she in a million after-school activities."

"Her grandmother signs her up in tons of stuff. She's going over to her grandmother's tonight. It's kind of the tradition. She goes on Thursday night and then stays until Saturday afternoon or Sunday morning if her grandmother wants to take her to church."

"Bummer. Well, I'll call her."

"Can I ask that you wait?"

"Why?"

"It's nothing wrong," he reassured. "It's just that I want you to myself. If you call, she'll come home tonight." He pulled Asia into his arms again. "Stay with me tonight."

He unbuttoned the first button of her blouse. Then he unbuttoned three more in succession. He flicked open the panels of material, enjoying the view of her breasts encased in a black lacy bra.

He cupped them, rubbing his fingers over the nipples that had already responded by tightening into nubs. He popped the latch between her breasts and freed them from the confines. Their softness coaxed him into giving his undivided attention to each breast, kissing and drawing each nipple into his mouth with a hard suck.

Asia sucked the air through her teeth before throwing back her head and arching in a throe of passion. A longing that she'd muted for weeks wouldn't stay hidden. As she clutched

Trace to her breasts, she wanted to throw wide the gates of her inhibition.

"I want you here."

He groaned. "I have cases this afternoon to be heard."

"Good, then you'll be all the better for being a good and objective judge, fully satisfied and hopefully begging for more." She went to his office door and locked it. "I'd suggest you tell your assistant that you don't want to be disturbed."

He obeyed. "I think you only want me for one thing."

"Yeah, right now." She planted a wet kiss on his throat and started opening his shirt, barely containing her impatience.

He pulled the pins from her hair and ran his fingers through the lengths until it settled on her shoulders. "I liked the dominatrix look, but I find the softer look sexier."

"I can't believe I'm doing this." With a small giggle, Asia partially covered her face with her hand.

"You don't hear any complaints from me."

"But this is really bad."

Trace kissed away her protest. "Stop playing with me, woman."

"If you insist." She pushed him away and then undressed for him, tossing him a condom in the process. Naked and aching for his touch, she stood before him in only her garter, hose and heels. While he admired her, she also got drunk on the vision of him, erect and ready to take her.

"Come on, big boy. Lunch hour is almost up." She headed for the couch, but didn't sit. Instead she put one foot up on the sofa seat, offering an invitation that didn't require a response. He slid his hand over her butt and squeezed lightly. His fingers trailed from the cheek down her leg, encouraging her sensual response that didn't need the extra help. She pushed him down on the sofa and straddled him, settling herself on his lap.

He took her nipple in his mouth and played with her until

the need for him to please her grew overpowering. She held him between her hands, honoring all parts of him with long strokes. Always the gentleman, he didn't neglect her, rubbing his fingers against the moistened folds at the apex of her legs.

She opened his legs wider, welcoming the sensitive touch of his fingers as they explored her, touching, playing with her in a heightened erotic way. Her hips answered, pushing against his hand, seeking that attention toward her G spot.

Asia felt the pressure. She pushed his hand away and impaled herself on him without further delay. She rocked hard, back and forth, pushing and grinding against Trace, raising the level of their performance to a frenzied pace.

She bore down for her release, but Trace shifted and lifted her effortlessly before settling her on the couch. Then he drove deeper into her. She gasped with sheer pleasure. Her world was being more than rocked. She clasped her legs around his hips, closed her eyes and hung on to his shoulders as if she had stepped into a roller coaster at the top of the New York, New York hotel in Vegas. At the peak, she took a deep breath, wondering if her heart would survive the ride. Then the climax shot through her system. The roller coaster had descended with sickeningly fast speed. She buried her teeth into his shoulder to keep from screaming.

Her body tightened and shock waves of tingling nerves sped through her. She enjoyed the ride as she careened at breakneck speed around blind curves and sudden rises to the unexpected drop, when she managed a squeak instead of a full-blown sexual cry.

After he had released, they limply fell against each other. Asia had to will herself to get up and dress.

# Chapter 11

Asia took out the front door key and inserted it in the lock. She only had a few seconds to disable the alarm with the password Trace gave her. After quickly digging through her pocketbook, she found the small yellow sticky note in her pocket. She quickly entered the password and hoped to see the green light to alert her that everything was normal at the house.

The colonial layout of the house was pretty traditional. The foyer separated the living room from a large family room, which led to an informal dining area. The living room emptied into the formal dining room. Toward the back, the kitchen expanded to almost the width of the house.

Unlike Trace's office, the house was neat and clean, considering Hannah's temperament. Photos of the family were situated on shelves or on top of furniture. The various stages of their lives had been documented. The family unit was intact, happy and wholesome.

Asia couldn't help but feel as if she was intruding on something that was so private. She was the outsider trying to fit into this family. The attempt made her nervous. Was she adequate to step into the woman's shoes who'd been Trace's love, and had left him the beautiful gift in Hannah?

She'd promised to wait for Trace. But she wanted to skip out and head back to the hotel. There, on her own turf, she could have some measure of security until she found an apartment.

Sitting in the family room watching TV didn't help her nervous disposition. Maybe she could fix a surprise dinner. If nothing else, she would be occupied. Starting from one end of the kitchen to the other, she noted where the dishes, pots and pans, and pantry items were stored. The quickest thing she could make was baked chicken, since there was a tray already thawed in the refrigerator. Then she spied Spanish rice mix, along with a frozen bag of cauliflower-and-broccoli mix. She was all set and looked forward to crafting a meal that would surely impress Trace.

Trace swore everything was so bright, it was as if he was in an animated movie. His mood had drastically improved since the morning. He went through his work with such a perkiness that he earned the prosecutor's curious glance more than once.

Time dragged, but eventually he was done for the day. After getting an update on the next day's appointments from his assistant, he left the courthouse.

Although Asia was reluctant to take his key, he was glad that she finally agreed to do so. They could have gone to her hotel room, but he wanted her to see his home and how he lived. He didn't want her to be concerned that he had an evil alter ego.

Trace ordered Chinese food. By the time he pulled in to the parking lot, they had texted him that his order was ready. Armed with a hearty meal of fried rice, Kung Pao chicken and Szechuan shrimp, Trace headed for home. Although the savory meal filled his nostrils, eating food was not his priority. Quite simply he couldn't get enough of Asia.

He pulled into the garage, glad to see Asia's car in the driveway. The minute he opened the door that led into the kitchen, he smelled the tantalizing flavor of a home-cooked meal.

"I didn't know you were going to bring dinner. Why didn't you call?"

"Thought I would surprise you." He came over to her and kissed her cheek.

"Might as well set it on the counter. Now you'll have your pick over my cooking or takeout."

"I'm looking forward to seeing if you have any skills in the kitchen."

"I bet." She winked at him. "But I do have other talents."

He placed his hand on her hip. "I'd say you do."

She bumped him with her hip and shooed him to change.

Asia set the table, adding a few candles for a little romantic flair. The baked chicken came out perfectly with a nice golden tone. The Spanish rice didn't disappoint, with its fluffy texture. Now all she needed was music.

"Are you looking for something?"

"I wanted to add music to our dining pleasure."

"Not a problem." Trace walked over to the entertainment center and plugged in his iPod. In a matter of seconds, soft instrumental jazz piped through the small speakers that provided enough power for the sound to fill the entire room.

"This is beautiful," Trace complimented.

"Hope you enjoy it."

They shared the meal, making small talk about Trace's job. Then Asia filled him in on the details about her interview and the company. She'd just finished her meal when her phone rang. She debated whether she should answer, but since she wasn't at her apartment, she'd better. She ran over to her pocketbook to retrieve the phone.

"Hello," she answered with a rushed breath.

"Miss Asia Crawford?"

"Yes." This had better not be a telemarketing call wasting her minutes. Her finger poised over the button to end the call.

"This is Sarah Jones from AXL Health Services."

"Yes." Asia's pulse immediately spiked. She crossed her fingers and waited.

"We felt we had a great interview. I wanted to let you know that we have decided that you are our best candidate. We would like to extend the offer with an additional ten thousand."

"Thank you. I do accept." Asia finished the call, struggling to listen and remember. Most of all, she wanted to get off the phone and celebrate with Trace.

"I take it you got the job," Trace remarked after she ended the call.

Asia nodded. "I actually did it. Now I don't have to consider that second job offer."

"Toast?"

"We don't have *champagne*," she complained.

"I've got apple juice."

"That'll work."

They shifted from the dining room to the family room. Asia appreciated Trace giving her some time to get used to being in his house. They watched TV in each other's arms, enjoying the easy flow of conversation. Tonight she only wanted to be held as they caught up on each other's lives.

"You know, I'm afraid to *meet* Marge."

"She's a little prickly at first. I think it's because she's shy. But once you get to know her, she is a solid, good-hearted person." He raised up on his elbow. "But don't ever call her Margie. Then you'll see a side of her that's like an attack dog." He chuckled. "I often wondered why that version of her name got to her."

"Trust me. I don't plan to look at her in the wrong way."

"Really, she's not that bad. Hannah adores her."

Asia thought about her grandmother. She'd adored her. While her mother was goal-oriented and carried stress as if it was an accessory item, her grandmother had been a free spirit and a risk-taker. Many times when she'd had a difficult time with her sister or mother, she went to her grandmother for advice or solace. Somehow the largest problems didn't seem so overwhelming when her grandmother broke it down and showed her the way out of the quagmire.

"Why so sad?"

Asia inhaled, clearing away the thoughts. "I was remembering my grandmother. She died last year."

Trace pulled her closer. He rested his chin in her hair as he intertwined his hand with hers.

"You're tense. I can sense it when your body tightens as if on alert. I promise nothing is going to jump out at you." He raised her hand. "See, even your hand was ready to ball in a fist."

"This is a little heavy for me." She looked around the room that was home to a family that was hers.

"Don't overthink the situation. Let's take this one day at a time."

"I know. But I also know that you want—"

Trace kissed her, drowning away any further discussion. His mouth coaxed hers to relax, submit and welcome his entry. Her body pulsed like a finely tuned orchestra ready to intertwine with his mastery of her needs.

She could cry for independence all day, but after Trace would kiss her, she could admit to a chemical imbalance. Her thinking would grow fuzzy until she was sure her brain had entered a chamber of gelatinous goop.

His mouth explored a path along the side of her neck. Her pulse spiked and continued to spike as his tongue added a blazing trail. She arched back, controlled by her passion and the urgent ache for his touch.

"This is going to kill me. But I know you aren't comfortable with being here."

"How did you know?"

"I told you that I can sense it. I'm in tune with your body." He traced the bridge of her nose before planting a soft kiss on the tip. "I don't want you to feel stressed. I know you've sacrificed a lot to come out here. And you have to do things on your own." He took her hand and kissed each finger. "But I am here for you. And will always be here for you."

Asia let the message sink in. Of course, Trace really didn't mean *always* in the strictest sense. He was so romantic that she expected him to say something sweet.

"Will you stay the night?" Trace asked.

"I think that I have to be sure that I'm forgiven by Hannah."

"She'll be home over the weekend." He explained the tradition he had with her grandmother.

"I won't mind if you wanted to call her tonight to see if she wanted to come home."

Trace nodded, and a small frown worked on his forehead.

"But either way, if she came home or not, I don't think I should stay." She sat up, but turned to face him. "I want to be a good role model to Hannah."

"She looks up to you," Trace added. "I'm glad to see this."

"It's good on one hand. I'm flattered that she sees me in that fashion. However, as we get closer, she may start comparing me to her mom. I can't live up to that ideal. Actually, I'm afraid to."

"I've deliberately kept Florence out of our conversations because I don't want you to think that I am seeking a replacement."

"I noticed. I know you've got memories that will always be dear to you and your family. I would never want to push those away. But I think Hannah may think that's what I want to do. I look around this home and see the success she had as a mother and wife." Asia exhaled, blinking back tears. "*Daunting* would be an understatement." She looked up at Trace, hoping he understood what she tried to say.

But he didn't say anything.

Instead he excused himself, got up and retrieved the phone. She heard him talk to Marge, then to Hannah. From where she sat, she could hear the young girl's scream. Knowing that Trace missed her warmed her in a deep, connected way, but knowing that Hannah missed her made her feel special.

"Marge and Hannah are on their way." Trace took her hand. "You don't have to be nervous. This has never been a competition."

Asia nodded, but he felt her nerves with the tightening grip on his fingers. "I need to freshen up." Now she had to meet Marge. She wanted every part of her to be perfect or darn close to it.

Trace pointed her to the room at the end of the hallway.

* * *

When the door closed, he resumed his seat on the sofa. He looked around the room, noting that not much had changed in the past few years. His desire to keep moving forward and deal with Hannah distracted him from anything else. Maybe it was time for a thorough cleaning and a complete makeover of the house.

The idea had substance. He grabbed hold of the possibilities, excitement building. And he would involve Hannah and Asia so that it would be their little team creating a home with a new feel. Maybe then, Asia could feel a part of the family. Hannah could build on the budding relationship. It would be a win-win situation, with having Asia within touching distance and keeping Hannah happy.

When Asia emerged, she looked happier. She'd dabbed on lipstick, the only prominent makeup that he could discern.

"Don't worry," he urged.

"When will they get here?" She walked to the window and looked out.

"In about half an hour, I suppose."

"How do I look?"

"Like a nervous Nelly."

"That's not funny." She smoothed the front of her blouse. "Maybe I should have worn a skirt."

"Yeah, then I would've gotten a chance to admire your legs."

"Stop kidding around, Trace. You don't understand how important this is."

"Are you always this high-stressed?"

Asia made a face at him. No matter what he said, she couldn't relax and smile. Now Trace got nervous, the mood catching on like a bad virus.

Maybe he should do all the talking.

\* \* \*

A short while later, Hannah burst through the front door. Asia opened her arms in ready welcome to the girl, who practically ran heavily into her. Asia scooped her up and spun her around.

"I missed you, chipmunk."

"I missed you, too, Asia. I kept telling Dad to call you, but he was stubborn."

"Stop telling her that stuff." Trace walked up and put an arm around them. "Where's your grandmother?"

"I'm right here." Marge stepped forward. Her gaze remained fastened on Asia. "Trace, I brought dinner for you."

"Thanks. I'll keep it for tomorrow. Asia cooked dinner earlier."

"Really."

"Marge, let me introduce Asia Crawford."

"Hannah filled me in." Marge stayed put, her pocketbook firmly clutched in her hands.

"How are you?" Asia offered her hand, almost sighing in relief when Marge stiffly shook it.

"Nice to meet you," Marge replied. Her cool assessing survey did nothing to validate her greeting.

Asia felt the icy path harden between her and Marge. Already uneasy, she didn't dare turn to Trace or Hannah for comfort. Then they would be in the untenable position of having to choose sides. No, this feeling of being accepted was hers alone.

"Asia, come up to my room, I want to show you something."

She followed Hannah, not bothering to ask for permission. Although Trace owned the house, his mother-in-law took over the room like the mistress of the home.

"This is my room." Hannah opened the door that was

directly opposite the flight of stairways. "I've got some pictures from Colorado." She ran over to her dresser and retrieved a small packet of photos.

"I didn't see you taking pictures."

"It's something I like to do."

The photos captured the unique, natural beauty with the ever-present mountains looming in the background. The vibrant colors and sharp images would make great framed pictures.

"You're good." Asia especially admired a photo where Hannah must have been perched on something high to get the unique angle. The young girl had talent to see the minutest detail in the wild and capture the skittish animals.

"I also took pictures of you and Dad."

"Really?" Asia ran through her memory bank to determine if there had been any compromising situations that Hannah may have captured.

"Here they are." Hannah rummaged through another drawer and pulled out a smaller stack of photos. She handed them to Asia.

"Why are they separated?"

"I keep my people-live shots separate in case I want to become that kind of photographer."

"Is that what you want to do? That's cool."

"Yeah. I was excited, too." She paused. "But Nana wasn't happy. She kept talking about my mother and how responsible she was at my age."

"Oh." Asia tried not to judge. Knowing that she hadn't gotten off to the best start with the older woman may have affected her reaction. "Grandmothers mean well."

"She looked at the photos, but didn't say anything about them." Hannah examined each photo, pausing over several. "I think they were okay."

"I'm impressed. I'm sure your father and grandmother were, too." Asia debated only briefly whether to come to Marge's defense. "Let me explain what your Nana may be feeling. You're like a one-story building. You can only see but so high and so far." Asia gestured with her hands. "Your grandmother, on the other hand, is like a skyscraper. Something that comes with years and life experience. Since she's standing so tall, she can see far and wide. She can spot the pitfalls and dangers that may be lurking nearby. And that's why she's pushing responsibility and all the lessons that your mother learned from her on to you."

Hannah nodded, then shook her head. "That means that she's too tall to see the good stuff on the ground. Plus she's blocking me from getting to be a skyscraper."

"How about, she just loves you very much and wants what's best for you."

"Now that's a Dad comment."

"Let's go back downstairs."

They walked into the living room, where a heated discussion between Trace and Marge was taking place. Asia paused, waiting for them to realize she'd entered.

"I didn't mean to interrupt. I'll be getting my things."

Trace turned to her as if ready to say something, but then decided against it.

"Trace?"

He held up his index finger, putting a halt to Marge's comments. Even if she wanted to ignore his finger, the expression on his face was enough to stop anyone.

"Don't mind me. I can see myself out." Asia grabbed her pocketbook. "Nice meeting you, Marge."

She hurried to the car, but not before hearing footsteps coming up behind her. In the car's window she saw Trace's reflection appear over her shoulder. She addressed him without turning. "What was that all about?"

"Don't worry, nothing crucial."

"Okay." She wondered if it was about her.

"Can you come over tomorrow for dinner?"

"Are you sure that's a good idea?" Asia tilted her head toward the house.

"I'm very sure." Trace kissed her softly on the mouth. "See you at six."

Asia nodded.

"I promise there will no drama."

Asia wasn't sure that his pronouncement would be true, even with his cross-his-heart gesture.

# Chapter 12

After Asia left, Trace reentered the house. No surprise to see Marge sitting in the living room waiting for him. The way she looked at him made him feel like a kid who had stepped out of line.

"Trace, before you close your mind to what I'm saying, let me finish. You're a busy man. You're rising in your career. On the other hand, you have Hannah on the cusp of being a young woman with no one to guide her. Yes, I'm here, but she needs much more than I can give her. The school that Florence went to is highly reputable, the famous alumni are still active and it gives her a chance to be around successful, upwardly mobile girls. Not the crowd that she'd have to deal with at that high school."

"I hear what you're saying but I don't think that this is the best time to send Hannah away. I don't want her to feel that I'm pushing her out of my life."

# Michelle Monkou

"That's nonsense. She's not a simple child. She will see the opportunity. I will help her see that this is best for her."

"Please, don't say anything."

Marge pursed her mouth, but didn't reply.

"Marge," Trace said, warning lacing his tone, "do not tell Hannah about this in any way."

"Fine. You need to think about why you are really holding her back. Is it for Hannah or for your benefit?"

Trace didn't want to continue the discussion any further. Marge had a way of twisting matters to conform to her logic. And he already felt guilty on a variety of things not to agree with her analysis. But no matter what, he didn't want to deal with sending Hannah to any school.

"Dad, I'm hungry." Hannah popped into the room, but stopped short. "This is the second time that I've come in and you all look as though you've been talking about me. What's up?"

"Nothing's up. We've got lots of options for dinner. Wash up, by then the food should be heated. Then I want to hear about school and the project you were working on for science."

Hannah heeded his request. He knew that she wasn't fully satisfied with his lack of response. She'd probably wait for her grandmother to leave before she tackled him with her questions. Who knew, maybe she'd want to follow in her mother's footsteps and go to the boarding school for girls.

Hannah returned from washing up. "I've eaten already, but I'll keep you company at dinner while you fill me in on your day." Trace pulled out the various containers of food and popped them into the microwave. Marge stepped up beside him to help. She offered him a small smile when he caught her eye. Looked like a truce would be called for the duration of the dinner hour.

As they took their seats, Trace wished that Asia had stayed.

But then, as always, he wanted the perfect scenario even in the most difficult circumstances.

"Dad, is Asia going to stay in Atlanta for good?"

"Yes, as far as I know. She did get a job offer today."

Hannah clapped her hands and gave a loud whoop.

"Please, Hannah, not at the table," Marge admonished.

"And school is almost over. I'm going to have the best summer."

"I've signed you up for horseback riding lessons." Marge beamed.

"Horseback riding?" Hannah looked doubtful.

"Try it, at least," Trace coaxed.

"Now, sweetheart, a young lady should know how to ride a horse correctly."

"Why? It's not like I'm going to take a horse to the mall."

Trace tried to hide his amusement.

"Don't be cheeky. Horseback riding helps with poise and grace. Something that you will not get in those baggy, misfitting clothes. Your mother shined as a horse rider. At your age, she'd already competed. I'll show you the pictures."

"You've already showed me the pictures." Hannah's familiar pout emerged.

"Well, this is my gift to you. You wouldn't turn down such a gift, would you?"

There, that was the classic Marge move. Trace needed to nip her manipulations.

"Trace, I've already paid the check. Classes will be every day through the summer. Horse riding in the mornings, then she'll learn how to groom and take care of the horses in the afternoon. I'll do the pick-up and drop-off."

"Thanks." He looked at Hannah stabbing at her piece of chicken. If he'd earned any cool points for getting Asia to Atlanta, they'd been stripped away with his surrender to Marge's summer plans. But he wasn't done yet. His daughter needed to have faith in Dad to come through.

Now pleased with herself, Marge got up and started clearing the dishes. She even hummed, happy that she had gotten her own way.

"Sweetheart," Trace said to Hannah. "I have a great project that I think you may enjoy. I think it's time to redecorate the house." Trace glanced around the room. "Furniture is a little tattered. You're getting older and your tastes must have changed. We might be able to use some of those tips off that TV show. What do you think?"

"Sure, Dad."

"Oh, come on, I thought you'd be thrilled." Trace thought he'd come up with a brilliant activity that would occupy Hannah and bring out some of her creativity. "What if we brought Asia into the planning, too?"

"Really?" Hannah perked up.

"I think that it's time that we do something fresh and new with the house. I was thinking of completely redecorating." He reached across the table and touched her hand. "So, what do you think?" Frankly he was surprised that he'd managed to get through the entire idea without an exclamation of joy.

"But makeovers tend to throw out everything and start fresh. There are things that are special to me. And some of them, Mom really liked or she was the one who did it."

"It's okay. Let's talk through everything."

"Let's talk through what?" Marge returned with a bowl of chopped pieces of apples. "You didn't have any of the usual desserts, so I had to go natural."

"Dad wants to redecorate the house, but it looks fine to me."

"I thought that we could update a few things," Trace explained.

"But this is the house that you and Florence picked out. Then you were so excited at moving from the town house. You all spent lots of time on getting it just right. Now you want to destroy it?" Marge looked over to her granddaughter.

"Hannah, think about it. You'd mentioned that you wanted us to get the marble-topped counter. I think if we did that, we might as well get the cabinets redone. And when we went to the home store last week, I saw the cabinets that would match the counter," Trace said, his mood shifting from panic to something lighter.

"Exactly. Then the floor will need new tiles."

Hannah pushed her chair back and disappeared out of the room. Her footsteps pounded overhead, then a door slammed. Trace didn't think he'd said or done anything to set her off. He breathed a sigh of relief when the pounding footsteps ran down the hall and down the steps.

"Here's the picture of what I think it should look like." Hannah shoved a glossy home-decoration magazine at him. Excitement shone in her face, infecting him with the same upbeat feeling.

"I think you've got something there. Asia would love to see it."

"We'll work on one room at a time." Hannah stopped talking and looked at him. "Dad, could we not do my room? Mom and I decorated my room. I may have to think about what I want to do."

"As you should," Marge piped up. She puffed her chest, full of anger.

"We can spruce up the paint, same color, to make it look fresher."

"Okay." Hannah appeared mollified. "I can't wait to start. When is Asia coming over again?"

"She might be very busy with settling in to her apartment. But I'll have her over soon. Maybe we could have a dinner party with a few of our friends to welcome her."

"Boy, that would be fun. I can plan it." Hannah looked over at her grandmother. "You'll help me, Nana, won't you?"

"Um…"

"Oh, please, Nana. You're good at all that stuff. You can be part of the team with Asia and me."

Marge squirmed in her chair. She fiddled with the dishes and silverware. Her mouth moved, but uttered no sound.

"It's good to see you so happy, Hannah." Then Marge looked up and Trace was shocked to see her teary-eyed.

"Hannah, I think your grandmother is a bit tired. You can harass her later."

"Okay. I'm going to go look at some pictures." She excused herself from the table, planted a goodbye kiss on her grandmother's cheek and left with the magazine tucked under her arm.

Trace waited until Hannah was out of earshot. Then he turned his attention to Marge. "Would you like some coffee?"

"Tonight, I will skip the coffee. I'm a bit tired." She blinked away any tears. Now the familiar formidable demeanor slipped into place.

"Okay, I won't push. Let me walk with you to your car."

She didn't resist his offer. They walked out to the car, where the outdoor lights automatically turned on when they passed a certain point.

"What's bothering you, Marge?" Trace noticed that Marge's pace was a tad slower. He positioned his arm for assistance, but knew better than to openly suggest that she may need help.

"I know that look. You use it when you think I'm pushing my nose into your business." Marge wagged her finger at him as he shook his head in denial. "My concern is Hannah, that's all. Are you sure you want to bring another woman in her life? What happens if it doesn't work out? What happens to Hannah, who always takes situations to another level? Are you ready to pick up the pieces when she gets disappointed? What happens when you get disappointed?"

Trace waited for Marge to take a few deep breaths. He placed his arm around her shoulders, calming her further. "You're asking me questions that I can't answer definitively. But no one can. I have to go on trust. I've got to live my life."

"Well, unfortunately my grief hasn't evaporated in the snap of a finger."

"Marge…"

"That's okay. I have my own demons to exorcise. Go give your daughter a good hug."

Trace allowed her to get in her car. He watched her drive away until the darkness swallowed her taillights. Under the balmy night, he took a minute to breathe. The entire day had been stressful in ways that he hadn't predicted.

Pieces of his life lay around him like a jigsaw puzzle. Assembling them into a coherent theme was proving to be difficult. Maybe he could be called greedy because he wanted it all—Hannah, Asia, Marge.

In the evenings, Asia sat in her furnished apartment with a few remaining boxes left to be unpacked. Some nights, she sat on her balcony watching the residents leave and enter the various apartment buildings. Her view split between the main street and the tenants' parking lot. The dark green foliage and large trees dotting the community provided a great backdrop from the busy downtown scene only a few miles away. From Chicago to Atlanta, the move had been a big impact on her life.

Even the sounds from the neighborhood differed—there was less traffic and she could hear sounds of children playing. The playground was off to the side of the property in a common area several feet from an apartment building. All in all, she was pleased with the six-month lease that she'd signed.

Asia couldn't believe a week was almost done at the new job. Starting work provided the perfect excuse to put a little distance between her and Trace. But the separation didn't stop her from thinking about him.

One afternoon, she gathered up her bag lunch and headed to the courtyard where most of the employees ate. Since she wasn't going to buy the expensive lunch, she had her tuna salad sandwich, chips, bottled water and an apple.

"Hey, Tina, wait a minute." Asia walked quickly to catch up to her colleague.

"How come you're eating so late today?" Tina had been with the company for five years. And in this first week, she had been incredibly helpful.

"I was working on that spreadsheet project. I didn't want to leave it until I got to a certain point. Now after I've eaten and rested my brain a little, I should be able to finish it this afternoon. Then I'll sleep on it and turn it in the morning."

"You're certainly getting the hang of it."

"Thanks to you. Can't imagine how I would have coped without you." Asia was truly grateful.

"No problem. We were all new at one time."

They chatted easily about the best place to work out, which

supermarket had the freshest foods and which pastor had the most uplifting sermons.

Tina looked at her watch. "Crap, I've got to get back. Meeting at one-thirty," she exclaimed.

"Have fun," Asia said as Tina left.

"Mind if I join you?" a voice said a few seconds later.

Asia looked up at the man standing at her table. She looked around to see who he may have been talking to.

"I'm talking to you." The stranger smiled.

Asia pulled her sandwich wrapper and other trash closer to her area. "Go ahead."

"I'm Bill Parker. I work in Administration."

Asia introduced herself, but didn't divulge which department she was in. From the look of Bill, he was a flirtatious, cocky man who had more personality than looks.

"Heard you are from Chicago. How are you faring in Atlanta? Need someone to show you around? At work? Or otherwise?" He smiled, slow and full of double meaning.

"Atlanta is fine. I'm getting the hang of everything."

"Heard that there're no family members here." He shook his head. "That's why having a base of friends is a good thing." Again, the sleazy grin appeared.

Asia shook her head. Irritation stirred that he had investigated her. Then he probably knew which department she worked in. But she didn't plan to give him any further encouragement. Being single in the big city was crappy, regardless of the geography.

"Here is my business card. A bunch of us go to happy hour on Fridays. It's a good way to meet a lot of the employees. Plus the place isn't a dive. Many ladies enjoy themselves. There is something like a fifteen-men-to-one-woman ratio in Atlanta." Bill snapped his finger and pointed at her like a gun. Then the glint of pearly white teeth flashed.

"Not my thing." She took his business card, but set it down instead of putting it in her pocketbook. "I'm sort of private."

"Me, too." Bill patted his chest.

Asia balled up her trash and then stood to show that the conversation had run its course. "Hang in there, Bill, I suspect that another new employee will be in need of your charm and contacts."

His smile drooped. A cold glint entered his intense gaze. "You can't go it alone around here."

"Thanks for the advice." She left before he could reply. She didn't want to have an exchange with him. She headed back to her office. Maybe she was being rough on the guy. If she wasn't involved with Trace, she might have been flattered. Slim chance, that, because she would have focused on career.

Now among mountains of spreadsheets, she had to come to terms with realizing this was her new home. And if she thought about it too much, she'd cry from homesickness and not seeing her sorors as often as she'd normally see them.

After work she felt drained. She wanted to head home and take a long shower. Her mood hadn't picked up after she'd thought about her family and her sorors. Not even a quick phone call from Trace was able to get her out of this funk.

She walked up to her car, noticing a piece of white paper stuck under her wiper blades. Her annoyance soared. "That bozo had better not be a relentless pain. I'll call HR on his butt so fast, his head will spin." She snatched the paper, ready to ball it up for the trash can. In neat, familiar handwriting, she saw her name.

Hi babe, I'm ready to return the favor of a home-cooked meal. Your place or mine.

She looked around to see if Trace was hiding in the vicinity. But there was no sign of him. She decided to call.

"Hey, got your note."

"What will it be?"

"I pick my place."

"Sounds fantastic. I'll get there around six-thirty."

"Great, my appetite will be waiting for you."

"Only your appetite?"

"Well, I didn't say which one, did I?"

"Don't tempt me, woman."

That quickly, the easy bantering gave way to lots of sexual innuendo. Maybe because they hadn't made love in a while, what with the constant reminders of his wife and Hannah's presence, plus Marge's habit of dropping in. Despite his culinary skills, she had ulterior motives for having him come to her house.

Asia was excited that Trace was coming for dinner. He'd come over to her apartment once, but only visited briefly. She wanted everything to be perfect.

While the chicken baked in the oven, she vacuumed the carpet and straightened the furniture, even putting fresh sheets on the bed. Good to be prepared on all fronts.

Before long the savory meal scented the place with promises of a delicious meal. She plugged in her iPod for a continual play of easy listening tunes, while she waited for Trace to arrive. And then it was time to wait.

Six-thirty turned into seven-thirty, then eight o'clock. Asia didn't want to seem like a nag, but called just to make sure he wasn't in an accident. Unfortunately she only got his voice mail. Instead she created a rhythm of checking her watch, looking out the window to the driveway, checking her phone line, then resuming her seat. Finally, she saw the headlights of a car flicker past her window. She jumped up to investigate.

She stood in the doorway. Her heart raced a little. Was he hurt? Was the car in an accident? Instead, he emerged with a wave and bright, wide smile. If she could wait to get her hands on his body, she'd slam the door.

"Glad you could make it…"

"I'm truly sorry." He presented a small brown teddy bear with a red bow. "A small token."

"Accepted." She also accepted the kiss that came with the gift.

"I had to wait for Marge to come over, then had to wait for her to be done with her concerns. We got into a discussion, or more like a lecture. I got caught up and didn't call." He shook his head. "Enough of that. My apologies to you. I want to have a wonderful night with you."

"I should have picked your place."

"Why didn't you?"

"Because I want to jump your bones. And I don't need to feel guilty, have distractions, or have a morality code killing the buzz."

Trace nodded. "Tonight's menu sounds fantastic, then."

"It's going to blow your mind." She sashayed into the kitchen to get the food. They exchanged easy conversation as she set the table. Trace fixed them a drink. As she breezed past him, he kissed her shoulder, ran an appreciative hand over her behind and occasionally tried to slide his hand up her thigh, if she'd let him.

"Let's eat."

"I'm looking forward to this. Frankly I'm tired of my cooking. Marge doesn't cook, she's got a cook. Plus her meals are microscopic. She's got the portion-size thing down pat."

"How's Hannah?" Asia didn't want to talk about Marge.

She hadn't broken through the ice cap and tonight wasn't the time to strategize.

"She's getting quiet again. But this time, there are no problems that I can see. The school said her grades are picking up. She's still not the most popular girl in the group. She's burned a lot of bridges, but she's also not engaging in any disputes."

"Could be a boy?"

"Hannah? Please. She'd probably brain me if I even suggested that she was having boy trouble."

Asia raised an eyebrow as Trace continued to reject the notion that his daughter may be turning her attention from hanging out with boys to liking them.

"Have you asked Marge, since they hang out together?"

"No. Marge is ready to ship her off to boarding school. If I suggested that anything was wrong, that I couldn't handle Hannah or know what was the matter, then she'd be ready to drive her there herself."

"Does Hannah want to go to the school?"

He paused. "You know, I never asked her."

Asia figured that subject was along the same lines as the topic of boys. Trace wasn't going to deal with it. "She's not fragile, you know?"

"I know my daughter."

"But you can't brush stuff aside. If you don't talk to her, someone else will. You may not get to approve the message or choose who that person will be." She couldn't believe that she sounded like her grandmother.

"I'm a better judge than a father." Trace ran a hand through his hair.

"I think you're a great dad. But you let those green eyes melt your heart. I avoid eye contact with her, so I'm not pulled in." They laughed. Asia continued, "Any objections if I talk to her?"

"No." He sounded relieved.

Asia got up to clear the dishes.

"Nope. I'll do that. You've done everything. It was all delicious."

"Okay." She sat back in the chair to watch him.

"Oh, no. You can wait in there."

Asia looked toward her bedroom. She grinned. "What's in it for me if I do what you say?"

He set down the dishes and came over. In a quick move, he lifted her from the chair and hoisted her around his hips. Then he planted a kiss, stimulating her down to her core. His tongue worked its magic, stirring her like a potent brew that took over her entire body.

He broke contact. His nostrils flared with his own reaction. His lips were beautifully sculpted. The words seemed distant. She slid off him in slow motion.

"I'll just go…wait," she mumbled. Her hand held on to the chairs as she walked into the room. She had to concentrate, putting one foot in front of the other. She felt drunk on the sexual potency of his body as she entered the bathroom.

She heard the dishes clanging as Trace cleared the table. From his hurried actions, it sounded as if he was loading the dishwasher. She appreciated his effort, but darn it, she didn't want to cool off. She cupped her hand under the faucet to catch the water. She drank, then patted her chest with the cool water.

She didn't know what was happening, but making love to Trace got hotter each time. Just as her heart opened up to him, her body wanted more of him—she had an intense need for satisfaction.

A dab of cologne on the back of her knees, and one at the

base of her neck, and she stepped out of the bathroom to take her spot on the bed. She'd barely made it under the covers when he came through the door.

"Dishes are done."

"Good. Now let me reward you."

"You see, this is where you've got it wrong." Trace undressed as he walked closer to the bed. "You've starved me for a number of weeks, more like a month. I'm not waiting for you to reward me. I'm a hungry man. And as such, I'm a dangerous man."

"Just making sure you're not taking me for granted."

"Come again?"

"I feel a little off-kilter, as if I'm running after you. I didn't want to be a matter of convenience."

"And now...?"

"I can't stand it anymore, I want you."

"Sounds like I'm a matter of convenience."

Asia nodded. She bit her lower lip and provided him with a slow, provocative wink.

Trace growled, sexy malice glinting in his eyes.

Asia backed up on the pillows. The dark glint in his eyes underscored the primal nature of sexual need. She'd had to fight her own urges and cursed her pride for not seeking him earlier. Now as he stood in front of her, aroused, as fit as a professional athlete and sexually charged, she had no more willpower.

"Stop talking, and bring it," she managed to say.

He lowered himself to lie between her legs. "This body is all mine."

She nodded. She just might need a glass of water to get through this onslaught.

She cried out with a gasp. Trace took her nipple into his

mouth and sucked it to attention, adding the soft flurry of strokes with his wicked tongue.

His hands rubbed the sides of her body. His thumbs took matters a step further to rub along her pelvic bones like an enticing appetizer before the main course. Her hips grinded against his, and she rubbed herself along his thigh. She was moist and ready. But he wasn't done playing with her.

Much to her satisfaction, he slid down her body. His hands now coaxed her breasts, tweaked her nipples.

She bit back shouting any obscenities, instead managing a loud hiss between her teeth. Her eyes closed. Her hands grabbed the sheets. Her toes curled. Her body contorted. Every muscle froze.

His tongue snaked a path down the middle of her body with a brief kiss on her belly button. But then he introduced himself to the part of her that ached for him to fill. With one stroke of his tongue against her clit, she arched back and raised her hips in easy compliance.

Not the shy one, he acquainted himself with every part of her. His tongue shared a dialogue so sensitive in nature that no interpreter was necessary.

"Please..." she begged. Her brain tried to communicate. Tried to tell him to stop teasing. She couldn't take another stroke of his tongue. She couldn't take any more deadly kisses. But her tongue, the traitor, wouldn't issue such commands.

"Shh..." He blew softly against the sensitive folds. Without warning, he entered her with his fingers, pushing against her.

He'd learned her secret spots. He'd mastered her body. He'd claimed every part of her. His fingers worked, inviting, manipulating. Her body, the apt pupil, answered the call with a tremble and a release that had her bearing down on his hand.

As an encore, he took her again with his mouth, loving her intimately in a way that brought tears to her eyes.

"Now let's make love until we fall asleep."

# Chapter 13

If he had to attend one more political fundraising gala he'd have a fit. Trace left his colleagues at the high-priced event, drawing more than his fair share of ribbing. But he didn't care. Life was settling down—not perfect, but improving on all counts.

Every night this week, Asia came to the house after work to go over the redecorating plans. Hannah was so excited when Asia was around that he barely got his daughter's standard hug. Although they didn't want his input, he still chimed in. Best of all, he enjoyed the laughter in the house.

"Are my favorite girls home?" he called out. The TV was on, but there was no sign of them.

He wandered through the rooms. Then he heard muted sounds of music. He grabbed a freshly baked chocolate chip cookie before he went on the hunt for them.

As he walked upstairs the music grew louder. He opened Hannah's door to see Asia and Hannah performing a duet on a karaoke machine. They hadn't noticed him, so he enjoyed the performance while munching on the rest of the cookie.

When Asia spun around for the final chorus she spotted him. A squeal of embarrassment erupted.

"Dad, you can't be spying."

"I was admiring. You sounded beautiful—not!"

Asia punched his arm. "I think since he wants to be so critical that we should put him to work."

"I've been working all day. I don't want to do anything."

"Oh, and I haven't?" Asia put her hands on her hips.

"And I had to clean out my lockers," Hannah said. To his blank stare, she added, "School's going to end in two days. Keep up, Daddy."

"So what do you want me to do?" he asked.

"We've picked the furniture. Done the research. And now you have to order it." Hannah presented him with their findings.

"How much?" he asked, after scanning the paperwork.

"Just a few thousand," Hannah offered with a grin. "You didn't give us a budget, although Asia made one. And we fit under our budget."

"Wonderful, how many digits were in this budget?"

"It has one comma, and that's all I'm going to say," Asia defended.

Trace excused himself to change clothes. He imagined that now furniture would be ordered, the painting would begin, and his home would be a whirlwind of action. But he looked forward to what it would look like.

With the new house, he wanted Asia in here as part of the family. Guess that meant he wanted to take things up a notch. He couldn't tell if she was ready to take that ride with him.


Later they played board games until Hannah had to get ready for bed. Trace laid his head on Asia's lap and they watched the ten o'clock news, commenting on the state of affairs on the national and local scene.

"How's the new job?"

"The newness has worn off." Asia laughed. "Lots of work, but I'm getting my feet planted."

"You know all I have to do is make a few calls."

"I know." Asia was tempted, but still resisted. "I will have to fly out for training at the headquarters."

"Where?"

"Chicago."

"Great. You'll get to see your family."

"I really miss them. I don't know how my sister manages being in another country."

"Why don't you invite them down here?"

"I wanted to get settled first."

"You mean you wanted to make sure that you and I were still together," Trace stated.

"Something like that. Colorado seems like a long time ago. In our paradise, the outside world didn't exist. We did whatever we wanted. Now we're back among the others."

"Yeah, I know what you mean."

Their conversation ended as they each drifted off into their own thoughts. Trace wanted more, much more. But he was so afraid to articulate his desire. He'd promised not to pressure or rush. But from everything he could tell, Asia felt the same about him. Yet, she didn't mention anything about being a part of the family.

Asia's stomach churned at the sound of Trace's car pulling in to the garage. She listened keenly to the door open, then close. The nausea intensified as she worried. She paced and wrung her hands, in complete distress. She took a deep breath as Trace opened the door leading into the kitchen.

"Hannah didn't come home," she blurted in one breath.

"What do you mean, she didn't come home?" Trace looked at his watch. "It's six o'clock. Why didn't you tell me?"

"She said that she had after-school activities." Asia wrung her hands. "Then I called Marge and she said that Hannah told her that we were going to the movies."

"Where's Marge?"

"She's on her way over here."

"If this is one of her crazy stunts, I'm going to throttle her."

Asia hoped that it was Hannah's mischievousness. Otherwise, the alternative was frightening. She could see that Trace's thoughts had already gone to that point. The time had gotten away from her because she'd spent so long looking for Hannah in the neighborhood, asking anyone if they'd seen her. She didn't want to have to tell Trace that his daughter was missing.

"Just called the police. They are sending someone over."

"Okay." As a judge, there were probably more heightened responses when something like this occurred.

Marge drove up. Her brakes screeched as she pulled to a stop. Asia didn't have time to open the door before the older woman came through. Her face was marked with worry. She wasn't dressed in her usual neat manner. Actually she looked normal in the sweatsuit, but probably on Marge's standards, she was a fashion disaster.

In a matter of minutes, two squad cars pulled up. Trace went out to them to make a report. Asia was left with Marge, the tension still thick between them.

"Has she ever done this?"

Marge shook her head. She kept her back partially to Asia.

"We just went to the movies and shopping this past weekend. She seemed quiet, and a little distracted."

"Then why didn't you tell Trace or me?" Marge turned toward her. "Trace and I have talked about the situation. He saw it, too."

"Well… I… Sorry." Asia didn't really know how to respond.

Trace reentered. "The police will check her room for any clues."

One of the officers bade a quick greeting and went up to the room. Trace followed.

"Why didn't Trace call me to watch Hannah? He always does."

"We were going to the store to pick out the curtains for the dining room."

"Oh, yes, I forgot, you're part of all this decorating nonsense."

"I thought you would help us. Hannah always talks about your interior decorating business."

"That was a long time ago." She sniffed, but then took a seat as primly as a queen. "My husband and I moved to Atlanta. He was an executive with a publishing company that is no longer in business. After we had Florence, I decided to use my fashion designing background for interior designing. I worked on many of the more upscale homes, making a name for myself."

Asia listened closely. Marge didn't reveal much information about herself, leaving her at a disadvantage on how to connect. But this little piece of news revealed more than a mother who gave her daughter and granddaughter everything she could. She saw a career woman with determination and desire to succeed, like her grandmother.

"We found something." Trace waved a piece of paper. "This must have been on her bed and fallen to the floor."

"What is it?" Marge asked.

"The note says that she's going to the hospital."

The officer immediately radioed in to check the nearby hospitals.

"Did she say why?" Asia tried to remember if Hannah had anything wrong with her.

"No." Trace turned the note over. "What on earth is going on?"

"They think that they've found her. She's at Grady Memorial. A young girl fitting the description came in, but wouldn't give her name."

"Has she been in an accident?"

"They didn't say. But I can give you an escort there."

"I'm coming," Asia declared, as she followed Trace to the garage.

"But, of course." He waited for Marge to gingerly make her way to the car.

Trace drove with Marge at his side. Asia didn't care where she sat as long as she went with them. Hopefully this girl was Hannah. Otherwise they were losing valuable time in searching for her.

The police escort made the ride feel as if it occurred in seconds. They hurried into the emergency wing of the hospital. Although they had a crisis, the packed waiting room highlighted the fact that so many others had emergencies.

"How may I help you?"

"We are looking for a girl who we think came to this hospital," the officer said, providing Hannah's description.

"Ah, yes. She's here."

"I'm her father."

"I'm her grandmother."

"First let's make sure it is Hannah." The doctor took Marge back, figuring that if the girl wasn't Hannah, seeing a female wouldn't terrify her.

Trace held Asia's hand. The waiting was unbearable.

"It's her." Marge beamed, her cheeks moist. The doctor stood behind her, also looking relieved.

Trace finished up with the officer. Thankfully the matter could be closed.

"What's the matter with her?" Trace asked, as soon as he returned.

"Come into my office."

They all squeezed into the doctor's office. Asia tried to read his expression, but the only thing she could tell was that he didn't seem worried.

"Hannah got her cycle."

"What?" Trace asked. "That's it?"

"Well, sir, it's a big deal. And no one had really talked to her about it. She knew that girls get it, but she didn't know the details."

"Oh." Trace shoved his hands in his pockets. "But she had her grandmother. And Asia."

"Probably that would have been fine, but then there was another issue. Apparently she was kissing a boy and when they hugged, her cycle came. She thought that he'd done something to make it come. She didn't know how to stop it. She didn't want you to find out that a boy made it happen."

"Doc, you're making my head spin."

"I think for right now she needs someone to understand what she's going through. She doesn't need to be lectured, as yet."

Asia felt sorry for the girl. "Doctor, may I see her?"

The doctor looked at Trace for his consent. He nodded.

Asia went to the area where Hannah sat huddled on a chair,

looking miserable. She was in her regular clothes. Her face was puffy from obvious tears.

"Hey, chipmunk."

"Asia?" She looked up and burst into tears.

"It's okay. I'm here to take you home."

Hannah wiped her tears. "Dad is mad, isn't he?"

"Dad is worried. But everyone is thankful that you're okay." She touched the tip of her nose. "You gave us quite a scare."

"Sorry."

"Ready to go home?"

"Can we go to your home?"

"Oh." Asia was shocked at the request. Hannah had never stayed in her home. She didn't know what Trace and Marge would think after this episode, and then say that she wasn't going home with them. However, she'd be Hannah's protector if it was necessary to get her through this traumatic situation. "I'll talk to your dad."

Asia left Hannah to find Trace. Evidently Marge had finished with her opinion on what needed to be done. Trace rubbed his forehead as if pain marked his brow. From the way Marge forced herself into his personal space, she could understand the source of his pain.

"Trace, may I speak to you?"

When he came over, she shared Hannah's request.

"This is unbelievable. Now she doesn't want to come home. I hope you told her that is not an option."

"Not exactly." She held his arm before he raised his voice any louder. "Right now she needs to talk. And we need to listen. You can lecture to your heart's content at another time."

"You're telling me what to do with my child?"

Asia recoiled from the accusatory, chilling tone. "I'm trying to help."

"You were helping when you took her shopping. You were going to get into her mind. But none of this you knew?" He threw his hands up in frustration. "And now she still wants to call the shots. I'm her father. I can't have her going off and acting out whenever she wants to. Doesn't work like that."

"She already did," Asia said quietly. "I need the time to talk to her without your anger over her head or her grandmother's criticism wreaking havoc."

"And what makes you an expert?"

"I'm on the outside."

"And that's where you'd prefer to be." Trace's gaze burned with a raging fire of anger. But Asia also felt the truth being told at the core of his rage.

"I'm not backing down, Trace." She was rattled. She had a frigid relationship with Marge. But with Trace, a fissure had cracked and opened slightly.

"Fine. But this is the last time anything like this will happen again." He pointed his finger at her.

Asia didn't respond, other than to breathe a little easier when he backed away to share the news with Marge. She expected to be verbally assaulted by Marge. Instead, a stony silence was her only punishment. She welcomed the punishment to be left alone.

On the drive to her apartment, Asia looked down at Hannah's head resting against her shoulder. At least one, very important, person in the car trusted and wanted to be around her. She liked feeling needed.

*Chapter 14*

Having Hannah spend the night was a treat for Asia. As Hannah took a shower after her long, eventful day, Asia threw a bag of popcorn into the microwave. She had a few sodas left and half a gallon of ice cream for floats.

Asia didn't push the conversation in any particular direction. Hannah knew she was there for her. Most of all, Asia wanted Hannah to relax and feel safe. There would be time for the lectures.

"Ooh, popcorn!" Hannah exclaimed, running over to grab a handful.

"Ah-ah. Get a bowl. Or else you'll be picking up pieces of popcorn from my floor with your fingers."

"Yes, ma'am."

Hannah's favorite rock group played in the background on the CD she'd supplied. At first, Hannah talked about school—which teachers she liked, which students she liked and what clubs she may enter next year at school. Then they started entering uneasy territory.

"Asia, what do you think about when you're with my father?"

"I think about so much. I think about how we met." She laughed. "I think about where we go from here."

"But that last one is an easy answer."

"Clue me in." Asia stopped munching to listen. She always marveled at how mature Hannah had become. And how difficult it must be for her to get the respect from adults, like her father.

"The easy answer is that you marry him."

Asia fidgeted under the simple solution. Honesty had its place. But she didn't know what she wanted and that was the honest answer. To say otherwise might mean she could be accused of leading Hannah down the wrong path.

"Don't you want to marry him?"

"I'm not answering any questions. I'm not the one to be interrogated." Asia took the detour around that hole.

"Do you, at least, love him?"

"Yes."

"Love is complicated. I thought that I loved Bruce. Or maybe I wanted to be kissed. When people think that you're a tomboy, then the girls tease, but the boys don't want to deal with you." Hannah scooted lower onto the couch. A yawn escaped. "Okay, I guess you have to tell me about the birds and the bees. I heard stuff. I've read stuff. Some things are gross. I want you to tell me without making up stuff because you think I can't handle it."

"Now?" Asia cringed at the image of her teaching sex education. Her problem was that she didn't know what was acceptable by Trace.

She grabbed a bowl, added two scoops of ice cream and

squeezed chocolate syrup over the top. This exercise called for high caloric reinforcement. She took a deep breath and resumed her seat, ready to begin.

Trace stood in the lobby, trying to remember what floor Asia worked on. He'd delayed going to the courthouse to catch her before her day grew busy. Until he figured out where he had to go, he'd endure the stares while standing in the lobby holding a bouquet of white roses.

"Sir, how can I help you?"

Trace gratefully looked at the security guard. So much for his surprise entrance. He provided Asia's name, along with his ID.

After checking with the receptionist, the guard shook his head. "Sorry, she's not in, as of yet."

Trace took the news, a tad disappointed. He took a seat in the lobby. Several women that passed made various comments.

"What a lucky woman."

"Got to call my husband."

"You must have screwed up big."

"Trace, is that you?" Asia hurried toward him.

He found the black pantsuit and crisp white shirt she wore quite sexy. She added height with a damagingly thin high-heeled pump. Only pearls dotted her ears and encircled her neck, simple and clean.

"I brought these for you." He shoved the flowers at her. He had a long apology worked up in his head, but the lobby didn't allow for that scenario.

"Thank you." She took the flowers. "Very nice. Very thoughtful."

"I wanted to say I'm sorry for how I acted at the hospital."

She raised the flowers to her nose and inhaled. She nodded with an appreciative smile. "You acted like a concerned father."

"I hear a...*but*."

"But sometimes you forget that it's not you and Hannah against the world, or for that matter, against me."

He sighed. "I got a little jealous of Hannah turning to you."

"Oh, Trace." Asia stepped forward, but became aware of her surroundings and stepped back. "You've got a treasure in Hannah. We underestimate how bright and intuitive she is. You have nothing to fear."

"I want to kiss you so badly."

"Trace," she warned as a smile tugged at the corner of her mouth.

"Please," he begged, enjoying teasing her.

"One quick—and I mean really quick—one." She tilted her mouth, but only slightly.

Trace stepped in to place a peck on her lips. But the closer he got, the more he wanted. By the time his lips made contact, he was a goner. He reached for her to halt any retreat and covered her mouth with a kiss to wake up her senses.

"You play dirty," she managed to say after fixing her smeared lipstick.

"All the time, baby." He grinned. Now he was ready to go to work.

Asia looked forward to milestones in her relationship with Trace. She'd kept her feelings of love from him, not sure if he'd been ready to hear such a statement before she left Colorado. Now they were together and working their way through the little hurdles that came their way.

But this particular milestone had boulder-size proportions.

If Hannah hadn't suggested her presence, she would not have volunteered to go to service with the family. Today wouldn't be any ordinary service, but a memorial to Florence, an annual tradition by the family.

Asia wore a deep purple dress, not sure what would be considered appropriate. Not only was she accompanying the family, but her position at Trace's side would also send a message that would feed the gossip mill. The pressure mounted for her to make a good impression.

She drove to Trace's, since the church was close to his house. Marge's car was already parked in the driveway. Her heart went out to the older lady. She wondered how she dealt with this every year and if it got easier for her.

She walked through the garage and entered the inner door. She spotted Hannah, who was dressed in a beautiful, floral print in a soft shade of pink. Her hair had been styled and a fringe put in place. She waved, but Hannah didn't wave back.

"Hello." She walked into the living room where they were all standing. Asia looked around to see what was the center of the conversation.

"Hi, babe." Trace kissed her cheek.

"Marge," Asia said, nodding.

Marge didn't respond. A tissue was balled in her hand. Her eyes looked puffy. Asia admired Marge's strength and faith to keep getting up and getting ahead.

"I still have to dress. I'll be right back." Trace exited in a hurry.

Asia didn't want to be left with Marge. She sympathized with the grieving mother, but that didn't mean that she wanted to hold any conversation with her. Marge's feelings had been pretty clear from the beginning. And Asia doubted that any thaw would occur as her relationship with Trace developed.

?

"Does Trace talk about Florence?"

"Yes. I've also asked about her. It's nice to have a tradition like this, especially for Hannah's sake."

"Yes, she'd be proud of Hannah. I will do my best to make sure that Hannah has the same opportunities as her mother."

"I think that is pretty smart."

Marge nodded. But Asia felt pretty sure that the older woman wasn't seeking her approval.

Asia looked at her watch, not really for the church service, but to time Trace's absence. She didn't know what to talk about with Marge. And anything that came out of Marge's mouth had an edge to it. Often, by the end of the day, Asia couldn't bear to be around her.

She pretended that she had to use the bathroom and excused herself. While in the bathroom, she took her time washing her hands. If Marge was this frosty, Asia knew that she wouldn't be sitting on either side of her.

She heard Trace's voice. Good, he had rejoined them. She touched up her makeup and exited the bathroom.

"I don't understand why?" Marge asked. The conversation was well under way without Asia.

"There's nothing to understand. I have a lady friend who I'm dating because I like her. Hopefully she likes me, too. Going to church for Florence's memorial is a pretty brave thing to do."

"I disagree with having her there."

"Then we'll agree to disagree. The bitterness is not healthy. I strongly urge you to attend church. Listen to the pastor. Allow his words to inspire you and heal the anger and hurt that permeates your life."

"Do you compare her to Florence?" Marge dabbed at her

eyes. "Because you can't. She's nothing next to her. She had style and grace. Could speak three languages."

Trace stepped in and pulled Marge into his arms. "I know, Marge. I understand your message. Trust me. I wouldn't let anyone into my family circle."

"And Hannah? She's at an age where she's a sponge. And she's attracted to people or things that thumb their nose at authority." She shook her head. "I think Asia Crawford is a bit unconventional. Why is she so interested in an older man and a child? I don't trust her. And I don't want her anywhere near my granddaughter. If you can't see people's true intentions, then you have nothing because they will take everything."

Asia waited for Trace to defend her. Instead he kept patting Marge's back, whispering encouraging words. His action melted away some of the anger that shot through her.

"Would I have a place in this family?" Marge asked.

"Always," Trace reassured.

"A new wife could change all of that."

"This is my house. You are my mother-in-law. Florence's passing shouldn't divide us or cause acrimony. We are a family," Trace said, his face full of conviction.

Asia had heard Trace say similar things to her. But when he said it to Marge, the message changed significantly. Again, that feeling of being an outsider haunted her. She could continue to look for proof, but it all seemed pretty clear to her.

# Chapter 15

Asia couldn't move even as she heard Marge storm out of the kitchen in her direction. She was stunned by the depth of Marge's misgivings toward her. And Trace didn't step up to support her. Instead he reiterated the fears that taunted her whenever she indulged in the fantasy of love and marriage with Trace.

Marge brushed past her.

Then Trace followed, pulling up short at the sight of her. "Asia?"

"Yes, it's me. Looks like I overheard some things I shouldn't have." Her voice shook a little. "I think that I'd better go home." She begged the tears not to make a presence.

"No. Please don't. We want you to go with us," Trace pleaded.

Asia shook her head. "I thought this would be really hard. And it is." She closed her eyes to think, to stay cool, to breathe. "This is a special time for the family."

"But you are family," Hannah said. "At least I think so. I know grandmother does, but she's hurting inside." Hannah put her arm around Asia's waist.

Marge stood at the door, waiting. Asia saw more anger than hurt, all directed at her.

"Please." Trace offered his elbow.

Asia complied. Thoughts brewed on an exit strategy. Trace's reassurances, coupled with these reality checks, urged a wake-up call. She had to fight against thinking that things could get better. Sometimes a relationship just wasn't meant to be.

Trace and Hannah separated her from Marge at the service. He was so attentive. She listened to the service, but was aware that she had only just entered the scene, and had interjected herself in the family. She'd enjoyed every minute of it, but what did she know about stepping in to raise a preteen?

Marge had had no problem letting her know that she was no match to her daughter. She didn't want to be, but on the other hand, she didn't want to be constantly reminded.

After church, they went to eat brunch at a favorite spot of Florence's.

"I can tell you're feeling awkward," Trace whispered.

"Just a bit," she lied. As they went down memory lane, she had to wait on the sideline. What could she contribute? Was Trace conflicted with remembering his wife, while she sat beside him? Her sorors had encouraged this as a sign of maturity and to show that she could adapt. Their advice sounded like psychological B.S. because she felt lousy.

Asia barely ate. She wished that she'd driven so she could escape right after lunch.

"I want to say a few things," Marge offered.

"Marge…" Trace's voice held a warning.

"I owe Asia an apology. I've been rude and unwelcoming. Truly, that's not me."

Everyone was stunned. Asia looked at Marge, wondering if there had been a body invasion. She couldn't respond.

"I listened to the sermon today. Remember when Pastor Chenault said that living without God's purpose is like existing in a barren desert? He talked about bitterness, anger and vengeance as the pills of evil that beat us into submission."

"It was pretty powerful," Asia agreed. The pastor's message continued with facing devastating fear. It didn't help that he seemed to pick her out from the third row to deliver the sermon. She would definitely read Matthew 10, as he'd urged the congregation, when she was alone. She shifted her attention back to Marge.

"I realized how fleeting life is. How much we hold on to people and things as if we have possession over them. I want my Florence back because I miss her. I want to tell her all the things that I didn't. I want to share my experiences with her to help her as she grew older. Now I want to do those things for Hannah. I know, Trace, you think that I don't think you're a good father. I've certainly given that perception on several occasions but that's far from the truth. You were a wonderful husband and you are a great father. All my actions are with the best intentions." She took out an envelope from her pocketbook. "Here's the acceptance letter to the boarding school."

"Marge…"

"Let me finish. I'll leave the envelope on the table. Do with it what you will. I'm going home now. I'm a little tired. I'm considering a cruise in Europe. It's time for me to trust that my daughter is alive in heaven." She got up from the table.

"Let me pay the bill and I'll take you home," Trace said.

"If you don't mind, I'll take a cab," Marge answered.

"Trace, take her home," Asia insisted. "Hannah and I will hang out at the mall." She leaned over. "Make sure she's okay." Asia couldn't believe that Marge had suddenly turned a corner. She worried that the woman may have surrendered in a way that was not healthy.

"No, we're all leaving now."

Trace took them back to the house. Then he followed Marge back to her home. Had he been so wrapped up in Asia that he missed the depression that Marge suffered? He realized now that she had been trying to tell him in her way how she had not overcome her grief. Since he had passed that critical stage, he falsely assumed that she had, too.

From his daughter's personal issues to his mother-in-law's emotional state, he felt like a lousy father and son-in-law. Asia had been able to step in when things got hot and messy and help with the solution. She did it repeatedly—and he loved her for it.

He got back to the house, excited that he was ready to make a commitment to Asia. He didn't want to wait any longer.

"Where's Hannah?"

"She's up in her room. Says she's ready to decorate."

"That's good news, don't you think? But I wonder if she's doing it because Marge's speech scared her."

"Or inspired her?" Asia offered.

"You don't believe that Marge has really moved on."

"Why not? She's not a fragile flower. And I think she's so embarrassed by her behavior that she served as her own wake-up call."

"Why are you so happy?"

"Because I was thinking about you."

Asia sensed that Trace was about to make a heavy statement. She backed up. Her mind was overwhelmed by today's events. Her thoughts were conflicted over her own inadequacies. She didn't want to hear Trace deliver anything that would rob her of the power to tell him that she needed a break.

"I love you, Asia."

He did it. He said it face-to-face. And her heart rejoiced as if a one-hundred-person choir sang "Hallelujah." But Trace wanted a commitment from her since they met. And with all the things pulling at his attention, the last thing he needed was to fire off a heavy declaration. After all, she had managed to keep her love sequestered.

"I see it in your face." Trace halted his celebration.

"See what."

"You're planning an exit strategy."

"Why would you think that way?"

"I know you well enough, Asia. Has nothing we've shared meant anything to you? Why would you throw it all away?"

"I'm not throwing away anything. You're being unfair and a bit melodramatic. I just think that you need to make sure that Marge is okay. You need to make sure that Hannah is fine with going to the boarding school if she wants to. You need to make sure that you are ready to move on with your life. You just need to make sure everything is okay." She breathed heavily.

"You can't keep running."

"Running? Look where I am. I'm in freaking Atlanta. How is that running?"

"I take a step closer and you take several back."

"Don't."

"I want you in my life. I know Hannah does. Marge made her attempts and I think that you should take it for what it is."

"How easy for you to talk and issue directives. Have you tried seeing things from my point of view? All of this is a little overwhelming. You've built your life with someone where you started out on the same level. You've set your dreams and already gone down the path to achieve them. I don't know how to weave myself into your well-established life. I feel out of step." Emotion welled in her chest, laboring her breath. She continued in a shaky voice, "How do I ask you to step back as I figure out what I want, where I want to go, how I may want to live?" She paused to halt any tears from falling. She didn't want to break down. "I don't know how to step in where all of that has already been done."

Trace pulled her into his arms. "There're no rules, Asia. No right or wrong. We struggle together, we celebrate together. Just because I had a family doesn't mean that I can't or don't want to experience life with you. And I will help you. But I can't do so if you walk away."

Trace wasn't giving up. He wanted Asia in his life. And he'd climb the highest mountain, cross a blazing desert, do anything to prove that he was worthy of her love. Fear had such a grip on her that he grew desperate in how to break through the binds.

He called her after work, when he knew she'd be home. "I haven't heard from you."

"Work got busy."

"Hannah's asking about you."

"Actually, I talked to her this afternoon."

"Oh. Why don't we have dinner this weekend and talk?"

"I'll be flying out next Friday, heading home for a few days to visit my family. So I'll need to run errands through the weekend."

"Well, at least let me take you to the airport."

Asia paused. "I don't want to be a bother. Besides, I've already arranged for a cab. I'll be on the two o'clock flight on NWATL."

"You weren't going to tell me?" Trace's hurt jabbed at her conscience.

"I just made the travel arrangements. I'm only gone for a short bit. Nothing dramatic. Why don't we plan for dinner with the family when I get back?" She aimed to calm any questions he was sure to toss her way.

"Sure. Do you want me to pick you up from the airport when you return?"

Asia accepted, hung up and took a deep breath. She hadn't lied about making the travel plans only a few minutes ago. Homesickness had a grip on her, along with the desire to see her sorors. She'd have to call to inform them of her impromptu visit. She knew they would take care of her doldrums with lots of laughter and TLC. When she returned, she would be ready to face a decision on her future with Trace.

Asia paid the cab fare after it pulled up to the carrier's departure area. As usual, Hartsfield Airport buzzed like an overblown beehive. How many people arrived in this city with lots of hope and dreams for a brighter future? She'd never thought of herself as a starry-eyed type. But love had a way of screwing with logic and common sense. She could barely contain how much she loved Trace and Hannah—even Marge had earned a warm place in her heart. Going home gave her a chance to make arrangements for the rest of her furniture to be sent, along with sharing the turn of events with her family and sorors. Atlanta would definitely be home for the near future.

Asia punched in the confirmation number of her e-ticket. Her name and seat number popped onto the screen. She acknowledged the information, including the number of checked luggage. Once she got her boarding pass, she waited in line as it snaked toward the security checkpoint. Her early arrival gave her enough time to deal with the crowds and long lines.

She had just turned down Terminal B and headed for the gate when she heard an announcement.

"Gate Twenty will begin boarding."

The announcement jarred Asia from a fast walk into a light jog. She had to switch to walking, however, as she encountered clumps of passengers who blocked her way. Missing the flight wasn't an option. Finally a clear path opened and she sprinted the last few feet.

"What rows have they announced?" she asked a woman waiting in front of her.

"Row twenty-six and higher."

Asia looked down at her ticket. She had 11A. On this particular airline, they boarded from the back of the plane. She'd flown other airlines that had tried the front-to-the-back boarding or by zones. Didn't seem to make a difference. There was always a bottleneck on the ramp leading onto the plane or in the aisle.

She waited off to the side as the vast array of passengers boarded. She had a window seat and her iPod. She could block out any chatty neighbor. If she closed her eyes, they would think she was asleep and leave her alone.

"Miss Crawford. Miss Asia Crawford, please come to the service counter."

"Now what?" she muttered, irritated that she had to leave her prime spot in the line to take care of an issue. "Yes, that's me."

"Ma'am, I need to check your ticket."

Asia handed over the ticket while the ticket agent typed incessantly into the machine. The queasy feeling that some-thing was wrong hit her. The woman shook her head, then showed the ticket to her colleague. Meanwhile, the crowd who waited to board slowly dwindled until the area was empty.

"Okay, looks like everything is fine. You may board now."

Asia took the documents, even more irritated with the woman, who smiled ever so sweetly. At least one of them was having a good day.

Finally she boarded and slipped into her seat. Traveling wore her out. She was glad the trip was just under two hours. Her nerves couldn't handle a long flight or hopping off one plane and hurrying for the next one.

Asia didn't wait for the flight attendant's advisory. She buckled her seat belt, turned off her phone and put away the iPod. Before long, the plane taxied down the runway, and took off sharply into the air. Asia offered up a prayer, just in case.

Once they hit the requisite altitude, the pilot stated, "You're now free to move from your seats. We should have a smooth flight."

The pilot's announcement didn't affect Asia. She rarely unbuckled her seat belt once the flight had commenced. However, she did reach for her iPod when the flight attendant allowed access to certain electronic devices.

"Ma'am, are you Asia Crawford?" One of the flight attendants tapped her on the shoulder.

"Yes, is there a problem?" Again. If this airline kept being a pain throughout her flight, she was going to write a complaint letter to the head office.

"Ah...well, we need to see your travel documents."

"Why?" Asia pulled her pocketbook from under the seat in front her. This routine was tedious. But she tried to stay calm before a U.S. Marshal or overzealous passengers restrained her for the remainder of the flight.

The flight attendant leaned forward. She dropped her voice. "We're having problems matching your seat number with what's on our manifest."

Asia frowned. She didn't understand the problem. But she'd rather try to fix it and get back to her seat as soon as possible. She followed the flight attendant to the front of the plane.

The slow walk down the aisle between rows of curious passengers didn't set her mind at ease. Instead her general irritation level rose, especially when the bolder passengers craned their necks to stare at her. Some had the nerve to giggle quite loudly as she passed. In a few cases, she stared them down. Her patience withered as the march continued.

"Would you tell me what's going on?" she asked as soon as she stood in the galley. The tiny kitchen provided false privacy, since she was sure the first-class passengers were now privy to the unwanted situation, along with her distress.

"Everything will be just fine," the flight attendant said. She smiled, a tad too merrily. Then she punched in the button for the PA system. "Passengers, good afternoon, it seems we may have a situation on board. Miss Crawford, would you please follow the flight attendant's instructions. Stand right there." Asia had no choice but to stand where the flight attendant firmly guided her by the arm.

What type of flight had she booked? If it was April, she would think it was an elaborate joke. If she was a celebrity, she'd think it was a prank. Instead she was simply Asia Crawford and now the entire plane knew her name.

"Look, I've tried to be patient, but this is ridiculous. My ticket was already checked. How many times are you going to check it?" Asia's temper flared.

The flight attendant only wiggled her head with the same perky, so-happy-to-be-alive type of smile.

"Trace Gunthrey, would you take your position, please?"

Asia looked around after the announcement. Didn't anyone else find this weird? Then she realized the name mentioned was Gunthrey. Trace was on the plane. Could it be her Trace? She spun around, craning her neck to find the familiar face.

"Okay, passengers of Flight 813, do your thing. On the count of three— One. Two. Three!"

"Asia, would you marry Trace?" The booming collective voice of the passengers, including the first-class and coach passengers, surprised her.

"Me?" She gasped. "Trace?" She turned to the flight attendant. "Please, where is he?" She looked down the aisle to see Trace standing at the other end of the plane in the galley area, similar to where she stood.

Now they faced each other.

Asia started down the aisle. She only wanted to be in Trace's arms. Seeing him dressed in dark slacks and a white polo shirt, hair newly trimmed, melted her heart. Many of the passengers seated in the aisle seats offered to shake her hand, along with providing several congratulatory remarks. Seeing his emotion swell easily brought her tears to the surface.

"Miss Crawford, what is your answer?"

Asia nodded.

"She said yes!" the passengers responded.

Trace smiled at her and she almost lost any semblance of sanity. She hurried to meet him as he matched her efforts to meet her.

When they connected, she jumped into his arms. The wild applause didn't stop her from peppering his face with kisses.

"I can't believe you did this. These people, the staff?" Asia could barely catch her breath. "Where are you sitting?"

"I have the seat next to you."

"How'd you manage this?"

"It took a lot of favors. Well worth it, though. I wanted to shout to the rooftops that I love you. I want you in my life. And we can make this work." Trace held her hand as they made their way back to their seats.

"Personally, I want to see this work," Denise said as she stopped by.

"Oh, my gosh, you're here?"

"So are we." Sara and Naomi waved from their seats a few rows back on the opposite side.

"Trace, you did all this?" Asia couldn't help being amazed.

"For you."

"He loves you, Asia." Hannah popped her head up from in front of them. "He told me so."

"Who else is on this plane?" Asia stood to see over the tops of the seats. Many passengers still wished her congratulations. She felt sorry for any who may've thought they'd be able to sleep.

"I am."

Asia turned toward the familiar voice. Marge was sitting in the same row with Hannah. Now she knew that she would lose it. Asia's tears flowed, along with Marge's.

"Make him happy," she whispered into her ear as Asia leaned over the top of the seat.

Asia resumed her seat next to Trace. "I'm ready to scale that mountain with you."

"I can't wait, because I booked our piece of paradise in Colorado to celebrate for the weekend."

Asia settled in the seat. She intertwined her hand with Trace's, enjoying his strength. Life was good.

# REQUEST YOUR FREE BOOKS!

## 2 FREE NOVELS
## PLUS 2 FREE GIFTS!

KIMANI™
ROMANCE

### Love's ultimate destination!

KROM10

# THE WESTMORELANDS

*NEW YORK TIMES*
bestselling author

# BRENDA JACKSON

## HOT WESTMORELAND NIGHTS

Ramsey Westmoreland knew better than to lust after the hired help. But Chloe, the new cook, was just so delectable. Though their affair was growing steamier, Chloe's motives became suspicious. And when he learned Chloe was carrying his child this Westmoreland Rancher had to choose between pride or duty.

*Available March 2010 wherever books are sold.*

**Always Powerful, Passionate and Provocative.**